Craving Vengeance
A Nick Spinelli Mystery

by

Valerie J. Clarizio

Published by
Melange Books, LLC
White Bear Lake, MN 55110
www.melange-books.com

Cover Art by Caroline Andrus

Craving Vengeance
Valerie J. Clarizio

Nick Spinelli's normal life as a homicide detective has been catapulted into a whirlwind of chaotic holiday adventures ever since he met the beautiful Shannon O'Hara.

Nick had hoped to spend his first Valentine's Day with Shannon in a traditional manner, starting with a nice dinner out on the town and then perhaps a long warm adventurous night in her arms. His plans quickly change when cupid is found murdered in a back alley. The investigation becomes more and more inconceivable, as Spinelli discovers that Shannon is linked to the victim. When another cupid turns up dead, and it is discovered that Shannon knows him as well, Spinelli is motivated to go undercover as a singing valentine dressed as cupid, complete with wings and a quiver of arrows. How many other cupids are at risk? Is Spinelli on the killer's list as well? The stress ignited by the day's events causes sparks to fly between Spinelli and Shannon as he struggles to piece it all together and stop the string of slayings.

Dedication

To my husband, Rick. Thanks for washing the dishes and entertaining the cat so I could lock myself in the computer room to write.

To my brothers. Thanks for the tidbits of male perspective you provided to me whether I wanted them or not.

A special thank you to my first critique partner, Virginia McCullough, who taught me about the craft of writing and red-lined my first manuscript more than I care to admit.

Last but not least, thank you Darla Tong for taking the time to read and re-read every manuscript I wrote until I got it right.

Chapter One

Spinelli's eyes popped open. He stared into the face of an angel. Was he still sleeping? How was it he had lured this beautiful creature into his life just a little over two months ago? He resisted the urge to run his fingers over her soft, milky white skin. She looked so peaceful when she slept. He would never be bored watching her sleep. Her slow even breaths mesmerized him. Was he dreaming? He almost went so far as to pinch his arm.

Shannon stirred and flipped over. Her shiny red hair spread out over her pillow like wildfire. He didn't need the nearby streetlight peaking through the window blinds to notice her fiery hair, but it certainly helped to illuminate its zest. Spinelli reached over and skimmed his hand over her soft hair. Silky strands sifted through his fingers sending an electrical current rippling throughout his body. He debated waking her, taking her again. He nearly chuckled at the thought. When they'd first met, they couldn't stand to be with one another, now they couldn't stand to be apart. Cupid's arrow struck him, hard and fast, out of nowhere. He was done, toast.

His cell phone vibrated on the nightstand. He reached over her to grab it before it woke her. Too late. Her beautiful emerald eyes fluttered open. He stared into the sea of green looking back at him, nearly forgetting about the call.

Her full ruby red lips stretched into a soft smile. "Nick, your phone is vibrating."

His ears focused on the sweet sound of his name rolling off her tongue. No one ever called him by his first name. Everyone called him

1

Spinelli or Detective, even Shannon did when they first met. But at some point over the past couple of months, she had started calling him by his first name. It nearly drove him insane every time she said it. His heart raced. He should take her again.

"Nick," she whispered, knocking him out of his reverie.

"What?"

"Your phone is still humming."

"Oh, yeah."

He grabbed his phone from the nightstand. The time in the upper right-hand corner read 4:00 a.m. Captain Jackson's face flashed across the screen. He tapped the screen and held the phone to his ear. "Spinelli here."

"Rise and shine, Spinelli. We got one for you, down on Water Street. Male, late 20's, cause of death not obvious. I've already texted you the address. The officers on the scene are cordoning off the premises."

Though he wasn't a morning person, not even close, a rush of adrenaline crashed through him like a tidal wave. This is what he lived for, catching killers. He sprang out of bed as Jackson's words trailed off. "I'm on it," Spinelli rasped before he disconnected the call.

He retrieved his contact list and tapped Detective Walker's profile. Walker answered with a growl. Spinelli gave him the details; then he did the same with Detective Marsh.

Spinelli slid into a pair of jeans and pulled a long sleeved navy polo shirt over his head. He grabbed his Beretta 9mm from his nightstand and secured it in his holster before he slung the chain connected to his gold detective badge over his head.

He'd nearly leaped through the bedroom door before he remembered Shannon still lay in his bed, entwined in his comforter. He'd rather it be that she were intertwined with him. He spun on his heel and in two long, quick steps was at her bedside.

Her bright green gaze fixed on him. An amused look covered her face. He knelt down beside the bed. "I gotta go."

"I gathered that."

"So I'll pick you up at your place tonight at 7:00?" he asked, confirming their dinner date.

"Yes...no."

Spinelli arched a brow. "No?"

Shannon rubbed her eyes. "I mean yes to dinner, but can we push it back to 8:00? I know that's getting late, but I'm scheduled to do the singing valentines for the church fundraiser from 4:00 until 7:00."

"Oh, okay. I'll change the dinner reservation."

He leaned forward and brushed his lips lightly across hers. He knew he had to keep it light or he wouldn't be able to leave.

She didn't play fair. She reached up, wrapped her arms around his neck, and pulled him to her. He let her, he was weak. His mind was mush.

He responded to her demand for more and deepened the kiss. His tongue passed through her lips. She tasted sweet. How did she always taste so sweet? His heart pounded in his chest.

Suddenly, Captain Jackson's words from moments ago echoed in his head. *We got one for you, down on Water Street. Male, late 20's, cause of death not obvious.* Christ, he'd nearly forgotten he had a dead body to attend to.

He pried his lips from Shannon's, nearly needing the help of a mechanic with a crowbar.

He rose to his feet, willing his knees to support him. She always left him weak-kneed, and she probably didn't have a clue. "I'll see you tonight. I have a special Valentine's evening planned for us."

* * * *

Shannon watched Nick walk out the door, sure that if he were to turn and look at her one more time with those dark charcoal eyes, she'd probably melt in an instant. He had the most intense eyes.

She curled into a ball and pulled the thick comforter up around her neck. His masculine scent coated the soft material, stimulating her senses, as if his mouthwatering kiss hadn't already left her completely aroused. She wished he hadn't had to leave. Another round of lovemaking would have been ideal. She'd had a taste of him, and now she couldn't seem to get enough.

She giggled at the thought of their rocky start. When she'd first met him she thought he was the most cold-hearted, egotistical human being she'd ever met. She'd never been more wrong in her life. He turned out to be exactly the opposite. Never in her life had she met anyone so caring, giving, and loving. His rough exterior was just a front he used to shield himself, as a result of his unfortunate upbringing. Growing up on the streets with a drug-addicted mother certainly took its toll on him.

A sense of pride crept through her as she thought about all he'd accomplished; finishing high school on his own after his mother died when he was only sixteen, then going on to college, and becoming one of Milwaukee's finest homicide detectives. It took a strong person to accomplish such. She admired his strength and determination.

Chapter Two

Spinelli pulled up to the crime scene to find Walker and Marsh already milling around. Several uniformed officers and a few plain-clothes individuals lingered about the area as well. Spinelli edged between his partners to take a look. "You gotta be shitting me. Is that Cupid?"

Walker nodded. "What gave it away? The nude man with wings, the bow, or the quiver full of arrows?" Walker asked.

"Very funny. What do we know? Has he been identified?"

Marsh smirked. "Hmm, I don't know about you, but I can tell you one thing for sure, I'm not searching him for a wallet."

Spinelli rolled his eyes and stuffed his cold hands into his pockets. "Are you two assholes about done now? Can we get down to business?" His breath fogged in front of him.

Walker cleared his throat. "A beat cop found him here, just over an hour ago, about 3:45 a.m. The cause of death isn't blatantly obvious. We'll have to wait for the pathologist's report. But judging from the vic's bluish-gray color I'd guess he's been here a couple of hours."

Spinelli glanced at the vic's body, as it lay lifeless over a small snow bank pushed up against a brick building. Ice crystals sparkled over his murky colored skin. The air temperature hovered around twenty-six degrees. With the wind chill factor, it was probably in the teens.

"Maybe the poor bastard was so drunk when he left one of the local bars that he passed out and froze to death," a nearby beat cop offered as he stepped closer to them.

Spinelli eyed the young cop for a moment. "Then what happened to his clothes? I'm guessing if he was in a bar, he would have been wearing clothes, right?"

"Well, maybe he was mugged, and they took his clothes and wallet," the beat cop stammered.

"So you're saying some thug happened by a guy passed out in a snow bank and instead of just taking his wallet, he stole his clothes, too? And then he intentionally left the wings, bow, and quiver full of arrows behind," Spinelli stated as he shifted his gaze to Marsh. "I suppose that makes sense. What do you think, Marsh?" Spinelli asked.

"I think I would have taken the wings. Chicks dig a guy with wings," Marsh replied.

"Dicks," the young officer mumbled before he disappeared into the crowd forming around the perimeter.

Though Cupid's body had been carted off, Spinelli, Walker, and Marsh lingered at the scene for a while longer, combing the area for evidence. Nothing specific presented itself.

The detectives returned to the precinct. It was nearly 7:00 a.m. Marsh made coffee as Spinelli hung pictures of the unidentified cupid on the crime board. He looked at Walker, "Not a good way to start Valentine's Day, having to tell everyone Cupid's been murdered."

Walker chuckled. "Yeah, now there's absolutely no hope at all for those poor souls searching for true love."

Marsh walked up and handed Spinelli and Walker their coffee mugs. Spinelli wrapped his freezing hands around the mug. His fingers began to thaw. Another minute or so and the feeling might actually come back.

All three detectives stared at the photos on the board.

"You know, the guy looks like he's about six feet tall or so and in great physical shape. It probably wouldn't have been easy for someone to manhandle him one on one. And there's no evidence of a struggle, either at the scene or on the body itself. The guy looks like he just fell asleep in a snow bank," Walker commented.

Spinelli yawned and skimmed his hand over his face. He didn't like getting up early. The nerve of someone, murdering Cupid on Valentine's Day before 8:00 a.m.

Spinelli cocked his head to the side. "I bet he was poisoned."

The others looked at him and nodded.

"It would be nice to get the pathologist's report. Spinelli, why don't you go down there and sweet talk Bethany into putting a rush on this case?" Marsh urged as a cocky smile stretched across his face.

Spinelli scowled at Marsh. He was probably the last person the department's pathologist wanted to see. He'd only gone out with Bethany a couple of times, but evidently she thought much more of the short relationship than he had. Now every time Spinelli had to deal with Bethany, she was colder to him than the mortuary cold chambers.

Spinelli's cell phone buzzed. He pulled it from his hip, tapped the screen, and pressed it to his ear. "Uh huh, okay. Hold on a second. Let me flip you on speaker so Walker and Marsh can hear."

They gathered around Spinelli's phone. The officer working the front desk continued talking, "We've got a young woman down here looking for her brother. She hasn't seen him since last night around 11:30. Judging from the description she gave, I thought he could be your John Doe from this morning. She brought a picture of him with her."

"I'll be right out," Spinelli replied before he ended the call.

Spinelli made his way to the waiting area. He glanced at the uniformed officer working the front desk who pointed at a woman seated in the first row of chairs. She stared out the window. Her hands nervously fondled the shoulder strap of the purse resting on her lap. She looked to be in her early thirties. Her dark brown hair was pulled back and bound at the nape of her neck, allowing him full access to her face. He knew already that the dead cupid was her brother. She resembled him. God, how he hated this part—having to deal with the survivors. He always got such an adrenaline rush when he nabbed the killers—he lived for it—but looking into the eyes of the survivors nearly kicked his ass every time.

He stepped toward the woman. His movement caught her attention, and she looked up at him through her long, thick lashes. Worry flashed in her eyes. She rose to her feet. Spinelli extended his hand toward her. "I'm Detective Spinelli. What can I do for you?"

"I'm Cindy Carter. I'm looking for my brother. I think something happened to him. He didn't come home last night," she said as she reached into the side pocket of her purse and pulled out a small photo.

Spinelli made no movement to take the photo. He already knew.

"Why don't you come with me, and you can tell me about your brother."

The woman nodded and followed him back to the detective area where Marsh and Walker waited. Spinelli glanced at their crime board. The pictures of Cupid had been removed. They walked past the board and into the interview room.

Spinelli gestured toward a chair and Cindy took a seat. He sat across the table from her. Walker and Marsh pulled up chairs as well. "Ms. Carter, this is Detective Marsh and Detective Walker. Can you tell us about your brother and why you think he's missing?"

"My brother's name is Mike. He's been living with me for the past several months because he was downsized out of his job about six months ago. Anyway, last night he left the house at about 11:30 p.m. which was unusual on its own, but it's even stranger for him not to come home at all."

Walker leaned forward. "How old is your brother?"

"Twenty-eight. I know what you must be thinking, but it's just not like him not to come home." Her eyes pleaded for belief.

Walker continued the questioning. "Did he say where he was going when he left last night?"

"Like I said, I thought it was odd that he'd be leaving at 11:30, so I asked him where he was going, and he just said out."

"Was he acting strange?" Marsh asked.

Cindy shook her head.

"What did he do before he became unemployed?" Walker questioned.

"He was a numbers analyst for a brokerage firm downtown."

Cindy pulled the photo from the side pocket of her purse and handed it to Walker. Spinelli and Marsh craned their necks to glance at the photo as well. It was Cupid all right, minus the wings, and bow and arrows. Mike looked all business-like in the photo, wearing a gray suit, white shirt, and red tie.

After a brief conversation with Ms. Carter, Spinelli knew Walker and Marsh were of like mind. She didn't have a clue as to what happened to her brother, nor any knowledge about any life-threatening activities in which he may have been involved.

8

Now for the hard part. Spinelli sucked in a breath and let it out as he captured Cindy's gaze. "Ms. Carter, we received a call early this morning about a homicide down on Water Street. I'm sorry, but the victim fits your brother's description, so I'm going to need you to come with me."

"No," Cindy whispered, and covered her mouth. Tears instantly ran down her rosy cheeks. She squeezed her eyes shut and rocked back and forth in her chair for a few moments before she opened her eyes and swiped her hands across her cheeks. She stared forward at the three of them.

"Ms. Carter, we need to know for sure. I need you to confirm the victim's ID. Can you come with me to do that?" Spinelli asked.

Cindy nodded slowly before she placed her trembling hands on the table to steady herself as she stood to follow Spinelli.

Chapter Three

Spinelli had just delivered Cindy Carter to the front door of the precinct when his cell phone rang. Walker's mug flashed across the screen.

"Spinelli here."

"Hey, you need to get back here. We gotta go."

"Why, what's up?"

"We got another one."

"Another dead body?" Spinelli inquired.

"Not just another dead body but another freaking dead cupid."

"You gotta be kidding me."

"Nope. Hurry up."

Spinelli met Walker in the parking lot where they climbed into their unmarked police car. He'd instructed Marsh to hang back to work on gathering and analyzing information about Carter. Perhaps he'd find something useful in Carter's financial records, or maybe one of the people on his contact list would be able to shed some light on what he was up to and what went down.

The morning traffic was terrible. It took them nearly thirty minutes to arrive at the crime scene.

A uniformed officer approached them the second they entered the bar. He pointed at a distraught older woman talking to another officer as they stood at the opposite side of the room near the entrance to a long hallway. "That's Gail Boyd. She's the cleaning woman. She found the vic in the office when she arrived at 8:00 a.m. The office is down the hall on the left, just past the bathrooms."

"Okay," Spinelli acknowledged as he studied the woman who looked to be in her late forties. She was of healthy size. She wore faded jeans and a dark gray sweatshirt. Her sleeves were pushed up to her elbows. Her eyes were red and swollen, and she'd obviously been crying for a while.

He and Walker headed toward the office and stopped in the doorway to take a look. Sure enough, there was another cupid sprawled out on the desk buck-naked. His thin, pillowed, satiny wings pressed between his body and the surface of the desk. The quiver full of arrows lay on the floor next to the bow. Just like the first dead cupid, this one was also a tall muscular man with dark hair.

"Jesus Christ. What the hell? Two in one day and on Valentine's Day of all days," Walker said as he eyed the dead man.

They stepped closer to inspect the body, peeking around Debra, the medical examiner. She glanced up at them, "Cause of death isn't blatantly evident."

"What?" Spinelli questioned as the acidic stench of vomit stung his nostrils and caused his eyes to water.

Debra looked up at him again. "He wasn't shot or stabbed, no sign of struggle. Judging from the vomit and strong smell of almonds, I'm guessing he was poisoned. Did you get any reports back from Bethany on the first cupid yet?"

"No, nothing yet. I'll talk with her when I get back," Spinelli replied as he shot her a frown. "You smell almonds?"

Debra arched a brow. "You don't?"

"Christ, how can you not smell that?" Walker questioned.

Spinelli shifted his gaze to the vomit splatter on the floor. "To me it smells acidic, almost tinny."

Debra shifted her gaze between the detectives and shrugged. "For some reason the almond smell associated with a poisoning isn't always evident to everyone. I don't know why, it just isn't. No big deal."

Spinelli and Walker went back into the bar to question the cleaning woman. She was still talking with the uniformed officer when they approached her. She looked a bit calmer than when they first saw her.

"Ms. Boyd."

"Yes."

"I'm Detective Spinelli," he gestured toward Walker. "This is Detective Walker. Can you tell us what happened?"

Ms. Boyd blew out a heavy sigh. "I clean the bar five days a week. I came in through the back door as I always do, and the door to the office was open. It's never open, so I peeked inside and found Tony, the bartender, sprawled out on the desk. At first, I thought maybe he'd just passed out or something, but when I stepped closer I realized his wide-eyed stare at the ceiling was that of a dead man."

"So you didn't see anyone else here this morning?" Walker asked.

Ms. Boyd shook her head. "Nope, just Tony." She shifted her gaze between them. "So you think someone murdered him?" she asked as her voice cracked.

"That's what we're trying to determine. How well did you know Mr...."

"Rosso," Ms. Boyd finished for Walker. "I didn't really know him that well. I'd see him sometimes when he opened the bar as I was finishing the clean-up. We'd chat for a moment before I left. He was such a nice young man. I can't imagine why anyone would want to kill him."

They asked Ms. Boyd a few more questions, but she wasn't much help.

"Ah, Christ, not on my desk. On all my papers," a gruff, smoker's voice bellowed from down the hall. Spinelli looked in that direction to find a large older gentleman standing in the hall staring through the office doorway.

"Sonny," Ms. Boyd yelled as she waved him over, "these detectives need to talk to you."

Sonny's head snapped in their direction. His jowls jiggled. He nodded and headed toward them.

"That's Sonny Tomes. He owns the bar."

Sonny waddled toward them. The cigar pinched between his teeth smelled sweet. Smoke trailed behind him. He pulled the cigar from his mouth. "Hi, I'm Sonny. What in the hell happened here?"

"That's what we're trying to figure out. I take it Tony worked last night," Spinelli inquired.

"Yeah, he was scheduled to close."

"Was anyone working with him?"

"No, it was a weeknight. During the weeknights, he closes on his own. Once we're through the happy hour rush, I go home."

"So you worked with him until what time?"

"I tended bar until about 7:00. Then I worked on paperwork in the office until I left at about 8:00."

"How was Tony last night? Was he acting unusual?"

Sonny paused for a moment. "He seemed fine. We were kind of busy, so we didn't talk much."

"How about the clientele? Was there anyone unusual or anyone acting different last night?"

Sonny nodded and smirked. "This is a bar. It's not uncommon for people to act strange."

Spinelli shot him a hard-eyed scowl.

Sonny shifted from one foot to the other. "No, sir. It was like any other routine night."

"Can you think of anyone who'd want Tony dead?"

"No…I don't know. He was just my bartender."

"We're going to need an employee contact list and a list of any of Tony's acquaintances you know of, including regular customers, friends, and girlfriend or wife."

Sonny chuckled.

"What's so funny?"

"If I knew their names, the list of his women friends would be extensive."

Spinelli arched a brow. "What do you mean by that?"

"Look at him. I hate to say it because I'm a guy and all, but Tony was a hell of a good looking guy. He did wonders for my business. I swear, all the professional women that work downtown came in for happy hour just to watch him work. Some of them hung around on occasion, if you know what I mean."

"I think I get the picture. Make sure to include their names on the contact lists."

They followed Sonny to his office, and he compiled the lists they'd asked for while the ME and her crew took Tony's body away.

Sonny pissed and moaned the entire time he drafted the list of customers. He set his pen down and hesitated for a brief moment before he handed the list to Spinelli. "Are you sure this is necessary? Do you really have to talk to all these people? Tony's murder will be bad enough for business as it is, but to question my regulars on top of it. I may as well hang the 'Out of Business' sign up right now."

Spinelli grabbed the list and stuffed it into his jacket pocket. He and Walker headed back to the precinct. They hoped to have some news from the pathologist about Mike Carter, their first cupid. With two murdered cupids, they were sure Bethany would be directed to make the cupid case her priority.

They also hoped to have some news from Marsh. Perhaps he found something useful about Mike Carter as well.

Spinelli shrugged out of his coat and flung it across the back of his chair. He walked up to Marsh's desk and looked over his shoulder to see what he was looking at. Walker did the same. Marsh pointed at the printout of Carter's bank record. "Look here. His account showed a decent balance for a middle income wage earner six months ago before he lost his job at the brokerage firm." Marsh skimmed his finger down the printout. "Then here, by month three of being unemployed, he blew through most of his savings." He slid his finger further down the page. "By month four there was pretty much nothing left, and that's about when he moved in with his sister. There wasn't any account activity from then until about a week ago." Marsh tapped his finger on the last deposit line. "Look at this, a $2,000 cash deposit all of a sudden."

"Where did that come from?" Walker asked.

"Good question. We can ask his sister if she knows anything about it when we go over there."

As they drove to Cindy Carter's house, Spinelli and Walker got Marsh up to speed on what little they knew about their second cupid, Tony Rosso. They decided they should pay visits to some of Rosso's acquaintances after they finished at the Carter house.

Spinelli dialed the ME. He thought it would be better to go through Debra rather than talk to Bethany directly. Bethany could sure hold a grudge. He feared even looking at her; he was certain her dagger shooting eyes would slice him into pieces.

Debra answered her cell on the second ring, "Hello."

"Hey, Debra, Spinelli here. Did you get Bethany's report on Mike Carter yet?"

"Not yet. I just got back. I'll head down there now and tell her what we found with our latest cupid. I'll see what she's found. I'll call you as soon as I know anything."

"Thanks." Spinelli disconnected the call.

Walker parked in Cindy Carter's driveway. She greeted them at the door. Her eyes were even redder and more swollen than when they'd seen her earlier. She invited them in and showed them to Mike's room. It was a small space. The bed was pushed up against the far wall. A nightstand covered with books and magazines, a reading light, and a TV remote stood next to the bed. Across from the foot of the bed was a chest of drawers. A small flat panel TV sat on top of it along with a jewelry box. Next to the chest was a small desk with a couple of drawers. His laptop sat at the center of the desk. Papers, envelopes, and pens cluttered the top as well.

The three of them and Cindy nearly filled the remainder of the room.

Cindy blotted her eyes with a tissue and cleared her throat. "As you can see, my house is small. There wasn't much room for Mike's stuff when he moved in so he rented a storage unit. All that's here are the necessities." Spinelli stepped toward the desk and then shot her a glance over his shoulder. "Would you mind if we took a look around?" They'd probably need to comb through the storage unit as well at some point.

Cindy nodded. "Go ahead. I'll be in the kitchen if you need me."

They went through Mike's meager belongings. They didn't find much in his desk either, just a few past due notices and some employment rejection letters. Mixed among the paperwork was an envelope with a Milwaukee County pre-stamped return address. It had already been opened and the contents removed. He glanced at the return address again just to verify its origin. At a fast glance it was easy to confuse the county and city pre-stamped envelopes. Definitely county. Curiosity nearly killed him. He set the envelope down and thumbed through the stack of papers again, looking for anything on county letterhead. Nothing surfaced. What had the county mailed to him? Spinelli couldn't seem to clear his mind of the empty envelope. He flipped through the papers again. All the paper shuffling released a familiar scent. Where was that aroma coming from? Spinelli inhaled deeply. The envelope? He picked it up again, held it under his nose, and inhaled. The aroma was strong. It was as if someone intentionally sprayed the envelope with perfume—not just any perfume but a familiar scent to him as well.

Walker craned his neck around Spinelli's shoulder. "What are you doing?"

Spinelli held the envelope in front of Walker. "Smell this."

Walker inhaled and shrugged.

"It's an envelope from the county."

"So?"

"Don't you find it strange a government envelope smells of perfume?" Spinelli asked.

"I guess."

Spinelli shifted, and held the envelope out to Marsh.

Marsh took a whiff. He didn't seem nearly as enthralled as Spinelli.

"It smells familiar to me, but I can't quite place it. Help me out, guys," Spinelli said as he sniffed at the envelope again. A hint of unease coiled in the pit of his stomach.

Walker and Marsh both shook their heads dismissively.

Marsh flipped open the laptop. It required a password to login. He looked as Spinelli. "It may take me a while crack this. Why don't you see if she'll let us take it back to the precinct?"

Spinelli nodded. Marsh was somewhat of a technology wizard, which was part of the reason Spinelli was glad when Marsh had been assigned to his team several months ago when his own partner, Mad Dog Maxwell, had retired. Spinelli had worked with Mad Dog for over six years. He really missed Maxwell, the mentor who taught him everything he needed to know about being a great homicide detective. But now Spinelli had his own team, Walker and Marsh, and things were working out better than anyone had thought they would. Spinelli was the intuitive one, Walker the analytical and politically correct one, and Marsh the technology wizard. There wasn't a case the three of them couldn't solve. But this case was moving fast, and they needed to get a handle on it before they wound up with another dead cupid on their hands.

They left Cindy's house and headed over to Tony Rosso's

downtown apartment located on the lakeshore in a high rise. The building was home to mostly upper middleclass tenants. Tony lived alone. Spinelli thought it odd that a single income bartender could afford such a place. It didn't make sense. *What was Tony into, beside bartending?*

The super let them in, and they milled around the apartment. Tony had good tastes. Large over-sized leather furniture filled the living room and faced a 60-inch flat panel TV. His marble-topped end tables were lined with bronze Roman warrior statues. A laptop sat on the center of the cocktail table. They'd take that back to the precinct and search its contents for anything that may lead them to the killer.

A glass case stood in the corner of the room. It was filled with swords. Spinelli didn't know much about swords, but he guessed they were expensive. They were displayed in velvet-lined holders and looked old.

A large aquarium lined the opposite side of the living room. It had to be at least a fifty-gallon tank. Spinelli watched Marsh as he eyed the bright colored fish. A few different species swam about. Marsh pointed at a bright blue fish trimmed in gold. "This is a Dwarf Angelfish. It would take about two weeks of my take-home pay to buy just one of these Resplendent Angelfish, and this bartender has at least four in this tank. Something isn't right here."

They snooped about the rest of Rosso's apartment. He had a lot of clothes and shoes, the expensive kind, not the kind one wears to bartend. Several thick gold chains hung on hooks just inside his walk-in closet. "If I didn't know any better, I'd bet that Mr. Rosso is a kept man," Walker joked.

Spinelli didn't laugh. Judging from what he was seeing, that statement just might be true.

Chapter Four

Shannon sat in her office perusing paperwork, incapable of any coherent thoughts. She pressed her fingers to her lips. They still tingled from Spinelli's early morning kiss. Though they'd been dating for over two months already, his kisses still had that effect on her.

She glanced at the photo of herself and Spinelli that sat on the corner of her desk. She picked it up and pulled it closer. The photo was taken last Christmas while they were working at the mall. Spinelli was wearing his Santa outfit and sitting in the plush red velvet chair in the Santa Village. Shannon stood behind him wearing her little red Santa helper dress trimmed with white fur.

She'd never forget the first day he played Santa Claus. The horrified look on his face was priceless as he studied the endless line of children waiting to see him. She giggled. He was like a fish out of water.

They'd met when he'd been reassigned from the Homicide Division to the Social Services Department to assist her with child recovery and placement for the holiday season. Both departments were short staffed, and neither of them accepted the assignment willingly.

He had no experience with children, and she had no patience for his unconventional ways. But when Santa Claus and an elf turned up dead, and she appeared to be next on the killer's list, it was Spinelli who came to the rescue. Without hesitation, he stepped out of his comfort zone, way out, and took on the undercover role of Santa Claus to keep an eye on her. Spinelli caught the killer, saved the day, and in the process, he captured her heart.

"Earth to Shannon, come in Shannon."

Shannon shifted her gaze up to meet her boss' eyes. "Huh?"

Anna chuckled. "Where is your mind? I've been talking to you for the past thirty seconds." Anna's eyes shifted down to the photo. She perched her hands on her well-rounded hips and smiled. "You're staring at that photo again?"

Shannon set the photo down, and Anna snatched it up. "Crissake he's good looking, even in the fat suit. And those eyes. He could talk a woman into anything without saying a word. I've never seen such dark, mysterious eyes. If I was twenty years younger, single, and you weren't dating him…well I'll just say he could eat crackers in my bed anytime."

Shannon rolled her eyes. "So what do you and Master Keith have planned for this Valentine's Day?" Shannon asked trying to divert the conversation away from her and Spinelli. She still couldn't believe they were a couple.

Anna sat. "Oh the usual, nice dinner at Samone's, probably the old fogey early bird special. And then reruns of Seinfeld or the King of Queens." Anna winked. "Maybe after a couple of reruns the little blue pill will have kicked in."

The women shared a laugh. Anna's husband, Keith, was as nice as they came but quite a bit older than she was. Dinner out on a work night was a big event for him.

"So what do you and Mr. Hottie have planned?"

Shannon thought for a moment as she recalled the intense look in Spinelli's eyes when he'd left her this morning. His words scrolled through her mind. *I have a special Valentines evening planned for us.* She couldn't wait to find out what he meant.

"He's taking me to dinner after I finish my singing valentine shift for the church fundraiser. Beyond that, I don't know. He said he had something special planned for us."

Anna leaned forward in her chair. "My God, do you think he's going to propose?"

"No…it would be too soon. Wouldn't it?"

Anna's smile stretched from ear to ear. "I see the way he looks at you. He eyes you up like you're his favorite kind of candy, and if I didn't know any better, your tone just a moment ago sounded as though you wouldn't mind if he did."

Shannon's breath hitched at the thought of Spinelli proposing. Adrenaline shot through her veins. Her head spun. Did she want him to propose to her? Was it too soon? Good God, she dove in head first on this one, so unlike her, but she just couldn't seem to help herself. She looked across her desk to find Anna's inquisitive eyes still fixed on her. "Jeez, Anna, I've never felt like this before. I can't say I would be disappointed if he did."

"Well, time will tell," Anna commented as she lifted herself from her chair. "I gotta get going. I'm meeting my sister for an early lunch."

"Okay, see ya later."

Shannon thought about Spinelli. She wondered if he was in the office, three stories below her, or if he was out in the field. She liked working in the same building as he did. It made it easy to pop in on him when she wanted to catch a glimpse of his magnificent, dark charcoal eyes, not to mention the gorgeous rest of him. But his eyes, those are what always caught her attention. Under the right conditions, they could melt her in an instant. Her breath quickened at the thought. Heat penetrated her body as raw need sifted through her. *Good God, Shannon, get it together. He's not even in the room.*

She fanned herself with a file folder before she flipped it open to study its contents. She needed to prepare for a custody hearing this afternoon. She dreaded going to the Clarkson hearing. Lamar and Chandra Clarkson, a couple of dope dealers, were seeking physical placement of their children, James, age six and Katrina, age three. Their last court hearing was nearly two months ago, and the judge denied the Clarkson's request for custody of their children when Lamar assaulted Shannon in the courtroom after her testimony. She hoped the judge would deny their request again. They weren't going to change, and she was sure they were probably still dealing.

Shannon closed the file, rose from her chair, and flung her wool coat over her shoulders. She planned to run up the block to Subway and grab a meatball sandwich for lunch. She stepped into the hall and nearly bumped into someone. He wrapped his arms around her, lifted her off her feet, and spun in a circle.

"Shannon, I'm so happy to see you."

She was speechless. She hadn't even seen his face, but she

recognized his hold, his scent, and his voice. Shock and excitement rippled through her like an electrical current.

He pulled his head back just a bit in order to find her lips with his. His kiss was rushed and firm at first but it didn't take long to turn soft and moist. Without conscious thought, she responded to his lingering kiss. Then all at once, her mind took over, and she realized what she was doing. She pulled her lips from his and freed herself from his embrace.

She stepped back and flung her hand over her mouth. Tears flooded her eyes.

He inched toward her, and she stepped back.

"Shannon, what's wrong? Aren't you happy to see your fiancé?" he asked as he handed her a fist full of roses.

She stammered. She couldn't seem to place her thoughts in order to speak even one syllable.

"I wanted to surprise you on Valentine's Day." His smile widened. "I'm guessing I succeeded."

Shannon looked around him to find Anna standing just beyond him, her chin nearly on the floor. He'd rendered them both momentarily speechless which was highly unusual, especially for Anna.

Anna closed her mouth and stepped forward. "Shannon, aren't you going to introduce me to your friend?"

Shannon cleared her throat and gestured toward him as anxiety churned in her stomach. "This is Dr. Joshua Meyers. Joshua, this is my boss, Anna Fontaine."

Joshua extended his hand toward Anna. "Pleased to meet you, ma'am." He shifted his gaze between them. "I'm Shannon's fiancé. She seemed to leave out that little detail."

Anna shook his hand. "It's nice to meet you, too," she replied before she shifted her curious gaze to Shannon.

Shannon fought the urge to immediately explain the circumstances to Anna. At this very instant she just wanted to get Joshua out of sight. "Anna, would you mind if I took a little longer lunch today?"

"Sure. No problem. Do what you need to do."

Anna spun on her heel and headed back into the office as though what she'd just seen had made her forget all about going out for lunch.

Shannon glanced at Joshua. He was smiling, his bright blue eyes twinkling. He winked. "You missed me that much, babe, that you need a little naughty afternooner right off the bat?"

Shannon perched her hands on her hips. "Somehow I don't think we're on the same page here. I think we need to talk. But not here."

She led Joshua down the back staircase and out the door to the parking lot. He reached toward her and wove his fingers between hers. She shook her hand loose.

He shot her a sideways glance and dropped his hand to his side. "Shannon, baby, what's the matter?" She refused to look at him. Apprehension squeezed her chest. She hoped nobody would see them together and tell Spinelli, but she was easily noticeable as she clenched a dozen long-stemmed, red roses in her hand.

Her pace increased. She needed to get to her car and get him as far away from here as possible.

She slid into the drivers' seat and slammed the door as Joshua climbed into the passenger seat. Shannon cranked the engine and pulled into traffic.

Joshua leaned toward her and nudged her shoulder. "Come on baby, what's the matter?" he asked again.

Shannon made an abrupt right-hand turn into a parking lot and halted on a dime in the far corner parking stall. Anger shot through her. Her lips quivered as she spoke. "What's wrong with me? You just announced in front of God and everybody that I was your fiancé. I know this may be hard for you to believe, but I didn't sit around waiting for your return for the past two years, just as I said I wouldn't when I handed the engagement ring back to you as you boarded your plane to Nicaragua. I'm in a relationship now with someone I love. What if your little show gets back to him before I get a chance to tell him about you?"

Joshua sat for a moment just gazing at her. The corners of his mouth began to lift upward. The smirk she'd grown to hate beamed radiantly. "I hear the words coming out of your mouth, but they're quite contradictory to the 'welcome home' kiss we just shared."

Shannon ground her teeth together and inhaled deeply before she loosened her jaw enough to speak. "You're wrong. That kiss meant nothing. I was caught off-guard."

* * * *

Spinelli reached into his pocket and pulled out the small black velvet box he'd picked up the day before. He popped it open and stared at the heart shaped solitaire diamond that sparkled like new fallen snow crystals. He snapped it shut and stuffed it back into his pocket. How could he have been such a fool? The stench of betrayal surrounded him.

He glanced back out the window from the fourth floor stairwell to find Shannon climbing into the driver's seat of her blue Chevy Impala. A strange man slid into the passenger seat. It was the same strange man he'd seen kissing her not five minutes ago in the hallway.

Aren't you happy to see your fiancé? The words echoed in Spinelli's head. Fiancé? What the hell? He should have confronted Shannon on the spot, but that word, *fiancé,* unnerved him. He heard it and ran for the stairwell before he threw up in front of them both. He'd gone to Shannon's office to see if she wanted to get some lunch with him, but that kiss and that word left him feeling like he might never eat again. How could he have been so stupid? How could he not have known she was engaged? And he called himself a detective!

He leaned against the wall. He couldn't seem to pull his gaze from them. He watched as they drove out of sight. His jaw clamped down so hard he thought his teeth might break. His ears hurt, and his vision blurred. Sweat slid down his back. What the hell just happened here? He thought Shannon was happy with him. She'd been with him every available moment for the past two months. Who was this guy, and where did he come from all of a sudden?

He blew out a heavy sigh and shook his head. He should have known better. True love, true happiness? Who was he kidding? Those things didn't exist for people like him. He'd learned that lesson long ago.

Chapter Five

Spinelli's phone buzzed. He pulled it from his hip to find Walker's face staring back at him. He tapped the screen. "Spinelli here."

"Are you about done with your lunch date?"

Some lunch date. Little did Walker know, he hadn't even had a chance to take Shannon to lunch because she was too busy feasting on someone else's mouth. Spinelli shook the vision from his head.

"Yeah, what's up?"

"You're not going to believe this, but we've got another one."

"Another dead cupid?"

"Yep, downtown at the Morgan Bank building."

Spinelli was already headed downstairs by the time he and Walker finished their conversation. He and Walker headed to the crime scene.

They took the elevator up to the sixth floor of the bank building to find several uniformed officers securing the area. Nearly the entire sixth floor had been gutted and was under major reconstruction. At least twenty somber looking construction workers milled about the site.

The Police Sergeant stood off in the corner talking to a large man wearing jeans and a plaid flannel shirt. His white hardhat looked squeaky clean, and his boots looked new, probably the job Foreman. The Sergeant waved them over. He gestured toward the beefy construction guy. "This is the project supervisor, John Buhr. He found the vic when they returned from their lunch break."

Buhr's head turned in the direction of the EMTs and the ME who'd just arrived. Spinelli could see a blurry rendition of them through the heavy sheet of plastic lining a small framed out room. Piles of sheetrock were stacked between where he stood and the room, preventing him from seeing anything below their shoulders. He and Walker headed in that direction with the sergeant and Buhr in tow.

They stepped around the sheetrock and peeked through the opening in the plastic. There he laid, cupid number three, naked as a jaybird with the exception of his white transparent wings. They looked like they were made out of a wedding veil and molded with large pipe cleaners. Spinelli had seen better wings.

The vic's stiff body rested up against bags of plaster powder. His bow and quiver of arrows lay next to him on the floor. Dried puke crusted in a line from the corner of his mouth, over his chin, down his neck, and onto his chest.

"Poisoned?" Spinelli asked Debra, the ME.

"Yeah, if I had to guess. The distinct smell of almonds kind of gives it away. Maybe by the time I get back I'll have the pathologist's report from Bethany for the first two cupids. I'll go see her right away. This is turning out to be quite the Valentine's Day."

Spinelli shifted his gaze to the floor. "You can say that again." Visions of Shannon kissing the strange man played through his mind. *This is what I get for letting my guard down. I knew there was no such thing as true love, and this just proved it. What in the hell was I thinking? Never again.* He glanced at the dead cupid. *And look at you lying there on the floor. What in the hell happened to you? A woman? Had to be.*

Buhr shuffled his feet, snapping Spinelli back into reality.

Spinelli shifted his gaze to meet Buhr's. "How and when did you find the victim?"

Buhr's eyes shifted from Spinelli to the victim and then back to Spinelli. He ran his hand over his large round face. "It was after lunch—about 1:00." He pointed toward the opposite corner of the large gutted room. "We'd been working over there since we got here this morning. There was no need to come over here. Anyhow, we broke for lunch at noon. We ate at the diner across the street. When we got back, I came over here to get some supplies, and I found poor Chad just lying here. I thought it was a joke at first, but it didn't take long to realize it wasn't."

Did Buhr really just call the victim by his first name? "You know the victim?"

"Yeah, it's Chad Williams, the city building inspector. He's been on the site several times already, and I've worked with him on other jobs."

"The building inspector," Walker repeated.

Buhr nodded.

"Did you all leave for lunch?" Spinelli questioned.

"Yeah. We don't usually eat on the work site."

"Did you all eat together?"

"All of us except for O'Neil and Crass," Buhr said as he pointed in the direction of the crew.

Spinelli couldn't really tell who he was pointing at, but he would surely find out which of the crew they were later. Then he and Walker would have a chat with them.

"Why didn't they go with you?"

"I don't know. They had some errands to run or something. They're not required to eat with us," Buhr said unable to hide the defensiveness in his tone.

Spinelli glanced toward the construction workers. "We'll need to talk with O'Neil and Crass. Which ones are they?"

Rather than answer, Buhr yelled across the room, "O'Neil, Crass, you guys need to come over here."

Every construction worker's head snapped in Buhr's direction, and then slowly most heads turned toward just two of the workers. Spinelli would have been able to identify the two even if the others hadn't zoned in on them. The second Buhr yelled their names the blood drained from their faces. O'Neil and Crass slowly walked toward him and Walker.

"Buhr told us you didn't eat lunch with the rest of the crew today. Is that correct?"

They both nodded.

"What did you do on your lunch break?"

The shorter of the two men spoke for the both of them. "We buzzed through the Burger King drive through and then went to the jewelry store to get Valentine's Day gifts for our wives."

Spinelli thought about the ring in his pocket for Shannon. What would he do with it now? A crater the size of the Grand Canyon filled his chest. *Damn it. Focus!*

"So you both were together the entire time?"

The two men nodded in unison.

Spinelli and Walker finished questioning the men and headed back to the precinct.

"Are you okay?" Walker asked as he wove their unmarked car through the heavy traffic.

Spinelli sat in the passenger seat staring out the front window. "Yeah, why?"

"You seem a bit distracted. And when those two guys talked about stopping by the jewelry store, your jaw knotted so tight I was sure I could hear your bones cracking."

"Well, we've got three dead cupids on our hands, and it's only 3:00. I guess you could say I might be a bit distracted."

"Nope, that's not it," Walker responded as he signaled and turned left.

"What?"

"Nice try but we both know murder doesn't affect you like that," Walker said as a chuckle escaped his lips, "and don't forget, I'm a trained observer."

Spinelli sat silent.

"So, how's Shannon? What have you got planned for tonight?" Walker asked.

Spinelli's jaw clenched. "She's fine, and I plan on catching a killer," he spoke through gritted teeth.

Walker parked in the back lot of the precinct.

Chapter Six

Spinelli flung his coat over the back of his desk chair and sauntered over to Marsh's desk. He looked over his shoulder as he sifted through files on Tony Rosso's laptop. Marsh pointed at the screen. "Look at this."

Walker stepped up behind Marsh as well. "What's that?" he asked.

"Rosso's bank records. How is it that a bartender has over $20,000 in his checkbook and nearly $300,000 in his mutual fund, especially when he's paying an arm and a leg for his fancy high-rise apartment on the waterfront?"

"What is he into?" Spinelli asked.

"That's the million dollar question," Marsh replied

Spinelli's phone buzzed. He yanked it from its holder. "Spinelli here."

"I've got the pathologist report from Bethany for your first two victims. Cause of death is cyanide poisoning. I can only guess, but I bet your third cupid's report will come back the same."

"Hmm, cyanide. I wonder why cyanide."

"It's highly toxic, almost always deadly, and works quickly, especially if ingested like it was."

"They ate it?"

"Looks like it. I can't say they knew they ate it, but they did."

"Interesting."

Spinelli disconnected the call and filled Walker and Marsh in on the details.

The three of them eyed the pictures of the dead cupids hanging on the crime board. They noted the similarities. All of the victims were slightly over six feet tall weighing in at 190 to 200 pounds, and they all sported thick, dark brown hair. Spinelli wasn't sure if any this meant anything, but it was all they had to go on at the moment. Marsh had been unable to turn up any other commonalities between Mike Carter and Tony Rosso based upon their contact lists, financials, and computer records. Maybe something would turn up when he cross-referenced their information with that of Chad Williams, their third and hopefully last dead cupid.

Spinelli's cell phone hummed. He pulled it from its holder and glanced at the display. Shannon's sparkling gaze stared back at him. He sent the call to voicemail. He caught Walker looking at the display as well.

"Not taking that?" Walker asked.

"It can wait," Spinelli said as he placed the phone back in its holder. He wasn't ready to talk to her yet. He needed to get his thoughts in order before he confronted her, but the cupid case prevented him from doing so. Maybe he'd never be ready to talk to her. He shook his head. *Freaking women.*

Spinelli shifted his gaze to Marsh. "Tell me about Cupid."

Marsh shot him a frown. "What?"

"Cupid, in general, what's the deal with this cupid character? You know, historically. Maybe we can find some sort of connection there."

"How the hell should I know?" Marsh questioned.

"You always seem to know this kind of useless information."

"Cupid is the son of Venus, the goddess of love, but I wouldn't expect someone like you to know anything about that," Bethany's shrill voice sounded behind Spinelli.

A chill raced down Spinelli's spine. His body tensed. What was she doing up here? He dreaded having to face her. She hated him with a passion. He never meant to hurt her, but it just wasn't there for him. Spinelli spun on his heel, "Bethany."

"Detective," she responded in a tone so cold dry ice would have warmed it.

He caught the glances exchanged between Walker and Marsh. He suspected that they probably wanted to disappear as well.

Bethany pressed on. "Supposedly, a person who is shot by cupid's golden arrow is filled with uncontrollable desire. I doubt that even cupid's arrow could penetrate your exterior."

Marsh chuckled.

Her angry gaze shifted to him. "What in the hell are you laughing at, Marsh? You're no better," Bethany snapped.

He pinched his lips together.

God, she's bitter. "Bethany, what can we do for you?" Spinelli asked in the softest voice he could muster.

She glared at him. "Nothing. I just thought you might want to know that Chad Williams was poisoned in the same manner as Carter and Rosso. All three ingested cyanide."

"How do you think the killer did it? Did he slip into a drink or something?" Walker asked.

Bethany shrugged. "Could have I suppose, or perhaps it was something they ate. All their blood alcohol levels came back negative."

Bethany stepped closer to the crime board and studied the photos. There were several photos of the dead bodies and one each of the men prior to their deaths. She glanced over her shoulder at the three detectives. "Have you guys noticed anything odd about your three victims?"

They all edged closer to the board. "What do you mean?" Walker asked.

She smirked. "They all look like Spinelli." She fixed her gaze on Spinelli. "Hmm. I wonder if that means anything. Might make for an interesting Valentine's Day for you. What kind of company have you been keeping?" Bethany questioned with a smirk just before she sauntered off.

Spinelli eyed the photos more closely. *What in the hell was Bethany talking about?* "Do I really look like them?"

"Sort of, I guess," Marsh responded. "Maybe I should cross-reference some of your lady friends with theirs."

"What?"

"Well, look how pissed Bethany is. Maybe we've got a scorned woman on our hands. Maybe she's trying to send a message," Marsh added as he pointed in the direction Bethany disappeared.

A hint of unease coiled in Spinelli's chest. Was Marsh right? Right now, his theory was as good as any. His mind drifted to thoughts of Shannon. *Freaking women! In the event they don't kill you, they stomp on your heart and tear you into pieces. I don't need this shit!*

Chapter Seven

The sound of high heels clicking against the old hardwood floor echoed in Spinelli's ears. A ripple of panic rushed through his veins. He kept his eyes forward staring at the crime board. Perhaps it was just Bethany again. He found himself wishing it was, but he knew the truth. He recognized the pace and the light steps. He willed himself to turn around, but he couldn't. It was as if he was frozen in place. He just couldn't face her yet. What could he possibly say to her? It was probably sixty-five degrees in the precinct, yet sweat beaded on his temples and upper lip.

Walker shifted away from the board. "Hi, Shannon. Happy Valentine's Day."

"Thanks, Brad. How's Jeana?"

"She's good."

Spinelli continued to stare at the board as he listened to their conversation. He shot a sideways glance at Walker and Marsh. Walker continued his chat with Shannon. Marsh looked like a starving wolf eyeing his prey. Spinelli wondered why he was looking at Shannon that way. She was probably just wearing one of her frumpy old business suits as usual.

Spinelli hated those drab suits. They made her look like an old maid, but he supposed they were appropriate for when she was working and had to go to court for child placement hearings. He remembered the first one he'd ever seen her wear. It was navy blue, and though it did nothing for her petite, yet shapely body, it did much more for her than the dark chocolate brown one she'd worn the next day.

"So, Shannon, any big plans tonight?" Walker asked.

Shannon reached over and touched the upper part of Spinelli's arm. His vision blurred. The photos on the crime board blended into one big, black mass. He'd thought he couldn't get any angrier. He was wrong. He still couldn't seem turn to his head to face her. She inched closer to him. The warmth of her body penetrated his. Her sweet scent filled the air, tormenting him. *Why is she down here? What does she want? Doesn't she know I know?*

"Nick is taking me to dinner tonight. What about you and Jeana? Any plans?"

Walker chuckled. "Yeah, we'll have our customary one night out for the year without the boys. Jeana's mom is coming over to watch them for a couple of hours."

"That'll be nice for the two of you," Shannon replied in her soft, sweet voice, which was normally music to Spinelli's ears. But today, right at this very instant, the sound of her voice was pure heart-piercing torture.

He imagined the sincere look in her eyes as she spoke to Walker. She always looked genuinely interested when she talked with people. *Hmf, sincere! Right!* Her soft feminine voice sang in his head. *Why did she always have to sound so sweet?* He found it difficult to keep his guard up. He thought about the ring in his pocket. It was of no use. He and Shannon would never have what Walker and Jeana have. He may as well just forget it and go back to the life he knew months ago, before Shannon invaded his soul. He slid his shaky, sweaty hands into his pockets and tried to re-focus on the photos of the dead cupids. The cupids were priority; not his messed up love life.

Shannon's grip tightened on his arm. His body tensed. "Nick, can I talk to you for a minute?"

Spinelli turned toward her. Speech escaped him.

"Are you okay?" Shannon asked, her tone almost a whisper. Her inquisitive, beautiful gaze fixed on him.

He needed her to stop looking at him through those long thick lashes, and he needed her to stop touching him. His aching heart couldn't take it. He stepped back. Her arm floated down to her side.

"I'm fine. I can't talk right now. We're in the middle of something important here. I'll talk to you later," Spinelli replied as he turned back toward the crime board. He just couldn't look at her any longer. And he couldn't help but notice the hint of hurt that flashed through her eyes as he spoke. Even after what she'd done to him, hurting her nearly cracked his heart in half. He raked his hand over his face and studied the board.

"Oh, okay, so I'll see you at eight. We can talk then."

Spinelli kept his gaze on the board. "About that. This could take all night. Maybe we'd better play it by ear."

Heat penetrated his shoulder blade. He imagined the source of the heat was her intense laser-pointed gaze. Any longer and it just might burn a hole through him. He heard her sigh.

"Okay," she whispered.

Her heels clicked against the hardwood floor as she walked away from him, each step fainter than the last until finally no clicking sound remained.

Spinelli felt Walker's gaze on him, and he was sure if Walker was speaking right now he'd be telling him what an asshole he was for treating Shannon so poorly moments ago.

"Jesus Christ, did you see what she was wearing? What's that all about?" Marsh asked as he stared in the direction Shannon disappeared.

Spinelli squeezed his eyes shut. Damn the convex mirror hanging in the corner above Marsh's desk. If it weren't for that, he probably wouldn't have noticed how sexy Shannon looked in that red dress. His heart nearly leaped out of his chest when he noticed, but then he remembered he was pissed at her. He was shocked nobody seemed to realize his gaze drifted to the mirror as he faced the crime board. If Walker hadn't been distracting everyone by rambling on about Valentine's Day, he would have probably been busted.

Her bright red dress was short and fitted. The hem fell right above her knees. He had noticed in the few seconds he'd spent facing her before she left that her low-cut neckline exposed just a hint of the tops of her soft, pale breasts. Her breasts were small, so he assumed she was wearing one of her sexy Victoria Secret push-up bras. He really liked the tiger print one. The dress had short, off the shoulder sleeves exposing her petite, well-toned, shoulders. He loved skimming his hands over her soft, milky white shoulders. He'd fought the urge to throw his jacket over her shoulders, imagining the other detectives might be eyeing her in the same manner as Marsh.

A wreath of tiny roses rested around her sassy up-do. Small clumps of curls hung down around the sides of her face and the back of her neck. To top everything off, she wore tall red boots with high heels. Nothing was sexier than a pale redhead wearing a bright red dress with tall red boots.

He thought about the night they'd shared last night. They'd made love twice, slowly and sweetly. She gave herself fully to him, and yet he could never get enough of her. Every nerve ending in his body lit up as her small, soft hands ran fluidly over him. And when he slid himself inside her, the soft velvet warmth surrounding him nearly drove him insane. He recalled how his body begged for release, but he fought to hold off until her pleasure came, making his pleasure even more erotic. At one point, they'd collapsed from exhaustion, rested for a bit, and then started up all over again. *How could a woman love a man like that and then kiss another, only hours later?*

Marsh slapped Spinelli on his shoulder blade, snapping him out of his daydream, but not before his thoughts had pulled a U-turn. His vision of Shannon suddenly included horns on her head and a devil's spear in her hand. Both seemed to accent the red dress as well.

"What?" Spinelli snapped at the touch of Marsh.

"I asked why she's dressed like that."

Spinelli shrugged. "She's doing some sort of Valentine's Day church fundraiser tonight. The proceeds are supposed to go toward the homeless shelter or something."

Marsh raised a brow. "Hmm."

"Hmm, what?" Spinelli questioned.

"I was just thinking that if I had someone like her waiting for me tonight, I wouldn't think twice about ditching these dead cupids and showing her what Valentine's Day is all about."

"How about we just focus on the case right now?" Spinelli replied as he crossed his arms over his chest and returned his gaze to the crime board.

* * * *

Shannon made it to her car on her wobbly knees without shedding a

35

single tear. She couldn't believe how cold Spinelli was to her moments ago. It's like he knew what had happened with Joshua earlier in the day.

She'd wanted to explain the whole Joshua thing to him before she headed off to the church, but he didn't give her the opportunity. And now she had to go and face Joshua again, at least for a few hours. Shannon sighed. Joshua was far more excited than she was to be working together tonight on the singing valentines and flower delivery fundraiser. Apparently, he'd made the request to Father Daniel that he be assigned to work with her, just like in years past. It didn't surprise her that Father would grant the request; he and Joshua were fairly close. And unfortunately, at this very moment, she was stuck, and agreed to meet Joshua at the church.

She started the car before she closed her eyes and leaned her head back onto the seat. She needed a minute yet. Visions of Joshua scooping her up into his arms and kissing her replayed in her mind. He'd caught her so off-guard. In fact, it happened so quickly she didn't even realize who'd scooped her up at first. But it took only moments to recognize his scent, his touch, his kiss. She blew out a sigh and fought the urge to smack herself in the head for having responded to his kiss at first, but when realization set in, she ended the kiss just as abruptly as it started. *No credit for that.* She'd give anything to start this day over again and change her initial reaction to Joshua's surprise visit.

She wondered if someone, other than Anna, had seen her and Joshua together and told Spinelli. She'd wanted to tell him herself, before anyone else had a chance, but by the time she'd returned to work from dropping Joshua off at his hotel, it was time for the custody hearing with the Clarkson's. She'd gone down to the precinct the first chance she had, but evidently, it was too late.

Shannon sucked in a deep breath and blew it out in an attempt to clear her mind. It didn't work. Probably nothing would erase the kiss she'd shared with Joshua or the coldness in Spinelli's voice when he spoke to her through his knotted jaw. *Why in the hell did Joshua suddenly show up, unannounced, after nearly two years on hiatus, and today of all days?*

She pulled a tissue from the box on the front seat and blotted her eyes dry, then swiped it over her cheeks. She checked her makeup in the visor mirror before she signaled and pulled out of the parking lot.

She arrived at the church at a few minutes after 4:00 and headed downstairs for her assignment. The sweet scent of roses greeted her in the cool stairwell. She stepped through the doorway into the social hall to find a room filled with red. Bouquets of long-stemmed red roses and red heart shaped boxes of chocolates covered the rows of banquet tables lined up throughout the entire length of the room. Sadness rippled through her. *Likely none for me today.*

Shannon always enjoyed spending time in the social hall. She liked visiting with the other parishioners as they congregated in the hall after the church services concluded. It was something she and her family had done ever since she was a child. Oh, what she'd give to have her older sister, Claire, here right now. Claire would know how to fix this mess with Spinelli. Why did she have to live so far away? Maybe she'd call Claire later, after her nephews went to bed so Claire would have time to talk uninterrupted. Shannon loved her nephews, but they could be quite the handful at times. She shook her head. She really shouldn't bother her sister on Valentine's Day. She might have plans with John, her dear, sweet husband. He was the nicest man. Shannon envied Claire when it came to her family. She always hoped to find a husband as loving and sweet as John seemed to be. Tears stung her eyes. *I had that man until I blew it today!*

Shannon blinked rapidly to clear her blurry vision. When the room came back into focus she found ten or so women, all dressed in red. They looked over their clipboards, which likely detailed their evening's delivery information. Shannon headed toward the table at which Father Daniel and Sisters Lora and Pat sat. She would get her instructions from them.

Men of all ages, sizes, and shapes milled about the room in their cupid costumes. They looked a little more like toga party goers than cupids, but the wings, bows, and quivers of arrows helped place their identity. Shannon giggled. She supposed the church couldn't very well send out naked cupids, as depicted in the legend.

She scanned the room for Joshua. He was nowhere to be found. She glanced at her watch. It wasn't like him to be late, especially for a church event. Shannon shook her head. He sure had everyone fooled, the good church-going Joshua. Mister 'I'll volunteer for the mission trip for the good of the church.' Even Father Daniel, still to this day, hadn't realized Joshua's true colors. Or maybe he did, and he was keeping him close to try to save him. Shannon sighed. She never quite fully understood where she'd gone wrong or why Joshua had volunteered for the trip when he did. She had loved him, and she'd thought he loved her.

They were set to get married and begin their new life together, but it didn't take long for her to discover his cheating ways. She'd even gone so far at the time as to work through the cheating issue, but she quickly learned she was the only party interested in making the relationship work long-term. She'd felt like such a fool when he told her he'd be going to Nicaragua, and then he had the nerve to suggest they could resume their relationship when he returned. It was as if he assumed she'd just sit around waiting for him, but how many other women would he tally up in that time? Her anger from two years ago roared through her as if everything had happened moments ago. *His parents should have named him Nathanael, the gift of God, because he sure thought he was God's gift to women! Why could no one else see this?*

"Hi, Shannon. Are you looking for Joshua?" Father Daniel asked as he stepped toward her.

"Yeah. Have you seen him?"

"Actually, I haven't. Not since he's been back. I wasn't expecting him back until next month, but I did talk to him on the phone earlier today. That's when I told him about the fundraiser, and he volunteered to work. Of course his caveat was that he partner with you," Father said with a sheepish smile. "I figured you'd be okay with that since so much time has passed."

"No problem. He and I talked earlier today as well," Shannon replied. What was she supposed to say? After all, it was for the good of the church, and due to the abundant number of clients this year, every available volunteer was a welcome sight, especially those with beautiful voices such as Joshua. Shannon recalled how his glorious voice always landed him the lead in the Christmas pageant before he'd decided to leave her and run off to Nicaragua with the mission group.

Father cleared his throat. "Yeah, I assumed you had. Joshua said he was going to pay you a visit at work." He shifted his gaze about the room. "I wonder where he is."

Shannon shrugged.

She visited with the others while she waited for Joshua. Several more minutes passed. Still no Joshua. She glanced at her full clipboard. The clock was ticking. There were so many deliveries to make and so little time. After a few more minutes, she and Father Daniel decided she'd better just get started on her own. There were no cupids left to help her.

Chapter Eight

Captain Jackson yelled across the precinct as she stepped through her office doorway, "Spinelli, tell me you guys have something on this cupid case."

He, Walker, and Marsh exchanged glances. He knew they were of like mind, wishing they either had something to go on or that they were anywhere Jackson wasn't.

Jackson walked toward them, her gait brisk. Her short brown curls bounced with every step she took. Her dark brown eyes fixed on Spinelli. Though she was a small woman, all of one hundred and thirty pounds, she managed to scare the hell out of him at times. Her twenty-plus years on the force had hardened her, but overall Spinelli liked her. She was smart, good at what she did, and fair.

Jackson stepped up to the board and studied the pictures of the dead cupids for a moment before she returned her gaze to Spinelli. "Well?"

He shook his head in shame. "Nothing. We've got nothing." He glanced at Marsh. "Marsh has been going through their financials, computer records, and contact lists but is coming up empty on making any sort of connection between the three of them."

Jackson inspected the board again. "So you think these are just all random cupids?"

"It's looking that way."

She glanced at the cell phone in her hand and tapped the screen a couple of times. "Well, maybe this will help," she said as Spinelli's phone buzzed.

He pulled it from its holder on his hip and glanced at the text message she'd just sent. "What's this?"

"The address of dead cupid number four. The call came through a minute ago."

"Son of a bitch," Spinelli growled.

He looked past Jackson to find Walker and Marsh staring back at him, their jaws nearly on the floor.

Spinelli and Walker drove to the crime scene. Marsh continued frantically analyzing the records of the murdered cupids. He needed to find something, anything, because four dead cupids on Valentine's Day, and their lack of finding the killer and preventing a fifth murder, made for an unwanted major news story. They didn't need any more bad press.

Walker drove toward the downtown Hyatt. He shifted lanes and glanced toward Spinelli. "Well, are you going to tell me why you were such a prick to Shannon?"

Spinelli stared out the window debating what to say, if anything.

Walker filled the silence, "In case you hadn't figured it out yet, she's a keeper, and keepers don't come around that often."

Just this morning Spinelli would have agreed with Walker. The ring in his pocket was proof. But now he didn't know what to think. He loved her, and even though they'd gotten off to a rocky start, he knew from the first moment he laid eyes on her, he had to make her his. He hadn't told her he loved her yet. They'd only been dating for slightly over two months. He'd planned on using the "L" word tonight. He thought she loved him as well, but seeing her kissing another man earlier in the day indicated he was clearly mistaken.

His chest tightened around his aching heart. His shoulders slumped under the weight he carried. Perhaps he should unload his burden and tell Walker what had happened. Maybe Walker would know what to do. He had experience when it came to commitment. He and his wife Jeana had been married for nearly ten years.

Spinelli's head spun to put his thoughts in order. He couldn't seem to find the proper words, even just for Walker. He normally liked to take the direct approach, but he wasn't sure he wanted to say the words aloud. The thought of actually saying them made it seem more real.

He stared out the windshield. Puffy snowflakes, the kind you get with a common Great Lakes-effect snowstorm, fell to the ground, making the ground look pure and clean. He once thought of Shannon as pure. In fact, in the beginning he thought maybe she was too pure and good for someone like him, but that all seemed to change about four hours ago. The windshield started to frost over. A moment ago he could see the streets of Milwaukee clearly, now he struggled to focus on them.

Walker pushed the defrost button. The windshield cleared. Maybe Walker had some sort of 'defrost' button he could use to help him see and understand Shannon's actions more clearly.

"Well, are you going to tell me or just sit there stewing on it?"

"I saw Shannon kissing another man who called himself her fiancé," Spinelli blurted before he turned to look at Walker who kept his gaze on the road. His expression didn't change. Walker was good at that. Even in crisis, Walker always looked the same.

"I see."

Spinelli's fists clenched. He sucked in a breath and expelled it. "When I went upstairs to see if she wanted to get some lunch, I saw her in the hallway outside her office with a man, Caucasian, dark hair, 5'10", about 170 pounds."

"Get a good look at him, did you?" Walker asked, his eyes unwavering from the road.

"It's not funny."

"I didn't say it was."

A few beats of silence passed.

"Are you sure?" Walker asked.

"Jesus Christ, I think I would know for sure if I saw my girlfriend kissing some other guy."

Walker inhaled and expelled a breath. "What I meant was, are you sure he said fiancé? Maybe it was just some old boyfriend bugging her on Valentine's Day."

"They were pressed together so tight I would have needed a crowbar to separate them. I'd say she was pretty happy to see him, and I know what I heard. He said, 'Aren't you happy to see your fiancé?'"

"The question indicates he wasn't so sure she was happy to see him. Maybe she wasn't. I take it she didn't see you."

"No. She was too busy."

Walker turned his head in Spinelli's direction. His look was sober. "You know you're going to have to talk to her about this, right? This doesn't sound like her. I'm sure there is a reasonable explanation."

Spinelli stared out the windshield.

"I mean it, Spinelli. Don't rule her out yet. Women like her are hard to come by."

Walker parked the car in one of the transient spots near the front door of the Hyatt. He flashed his badge at the valet. The young man nodded. They continued on toward the elevators and rode up to the sixth floor.

Yellow tape already cordoned off the crime scene. Debra poked her head out of the doorway of room 602. They ducked under the tape and entered the room. There he was, their fourth dead cupid of the day, spread-eagle on top of the bed, naked as a jaybird. His thin, pillowed, satin wings trimmed with gold colored garland were sprawled around him. His bow lay next to him on the bed, and his quiver of arrows leaned up against the nightstand.

"Can you believe this shit?" the ME questioned as she pointed at cupid number four. Her eyes focused on Spinelli. "What in the hell? How many cupids are left in the city?"

Spinelli and Walker stepped up to the bedside. A small round serving tray, two wine glasses—one broken—and a single long-stemmed red rose lay on the floor several feet from the bed. Next to the mess stood a shiny metal champagne chiller on a stand. Only the stem of the champagne bottle stuck out above the ice.

Spinelli shifted his gaze to the dead man sprawled out on the bed. His heart pounded against his ribs, his cheeks burned, and the air drained from his lungs. His throat constricted. He fought for a breath. None came. He tried again. He caught some air on the second go around.

He could hear Walker talking to Debra and the Sergeant, but his mind wouldn't process the words. He continued to stare down at the face of the victim. He couldn't seem to tear his eyes from him.

Walker tapped him on the shoulder. "Are you okay?"

"Yeah, I just…he just…has he been identified?"

Walker frowned. "Yeah, that's what the Sergeant just told us. The room was rented to Dr. Joshua Meyers, and he matches that of the picture ID in the wallet on the desk over there," Walker said as he pointed to the desk in the corner of the room.

"Doctor. That just figures," Spinelli mumbled as he tried to make sense of it all.

"What?" Walker asked.

Spinelli glanced at the Police Sergeant and the ME then shifted his gaze to Walker. He shook his head. "Nothing, never mind." He'd wait to tell Walker in private that the fourth dead cupid was the man he saw Shannon kissing earlier in the day.

"Debra, do you have an estimate as to the time of death or any ideas as to the cause of death?" Spinelli asked.

"Not long. Couple of hours, tops. Judging from the smell of almonds, I'm guessing we have another cyanide poisoned victim. He doesn't have any visible wounds."

A golf ball sized lump formed in Spinelli's throat making it difficult to ask the Sergeant his next question. "Did you talk to any hotel staff? Did he check in with anyone?"

The Sergeant pointed to the doorway. "The shift manager is in the hall waiting for you guys. Earlier he said that Meyers was alone when he checked in at around 1:45."

A wave of relief washed through Spinelli, but Shannon wasn't off the hook yet. Why was the man she kissed only hours ago now dead? And who exactly was this man?

They stepped back into the hall to talk to the manager. Walker introduced himself and Spinelli. "Hi, I'm Marcus Grasse, the front desk manager," Marcus responded in a shaky voice.

Spinelli's silence caused Walker to start the questioning.

"So, you said Dr. Meyers checked in alone," Walker stated.

The young manager nodded his head. He stood with his hands in his pockets and shifted from foot to foot, confirming his nervousness.

He looked to be in his early twenties. Probably his first real job out of college, and he winds up with a murder on his shift.

"Did you check him in or did someone else?"

Marcus shifted his gaze to the floor. "I did," he whispered.

"Did he say anything when he checked in or was he acting unusual at all?"

The kid chewed on his lip for a moment, then released it from his teeth. "It was like any other routine check-in. He told me his name. I punched it in on the computer and found his reservation. I swiped his credit card, handed him his room key, and gave him a map of the hotel."

"So he had a reservation?" Walker questioned.

"Yep."

"Do you know when he made the arrangements?"

"It was earlier in the day, actually, shortly before he arrived. We're not super busy during the week this time of year. I took the call myself while I was working the counter."

"Who found him?"

Marcus pulled his hand from his pocket and ran it over his face. He pointed at a young woman sitting on a bench at the end of the hall. She was talking with a uniformed officer who stood by the caution tape dividing the perimeter from the rest of the world. Even from this distance, Spinelli easily noticed her red, swollen eyes. She took a pull from a bottle of water.

The three of them walked toward the woman. She rose to her feet as they ducked under the caution tape. Walker introduced himself and Spinelli. Her frantic gaze darted between the men then landed on Marcus. He gestured toward her. "This is Ashley Dart. She found Dr. Meyers when she delivered the champagne and rose he'd ordered shortly after he checked in."

The young waitress swiped under her eyes with a balled up tissue.

"Ms. Dart, was anyone else in the room when you entered?"

She shook her head.

"So tell me how this works. You knocked on the door, no one answered, and you let yourself in?"

"Yes. When he ordered the room service, he specifically said he wanted the order brought up at 4:00. He wanted the champagne to chill on ice for a few hours. So I arrived at his door and knocked. He didn't answer, so I knocked again and identified myself. Still no answer, so I spoke through the door and told him that I was going to let myself in. I entered the room and found him," she sniffled and pressed on. "I was startled. I dropped the tray and ran out of the room. I didn't stop until I found Marcus and told him what had happened. He called the police, and now here we are."

Tears ran down her cheeks. "I don't know why I'm crying like this. I don't even know the man."

Marcus nodded.

"Did you see anyone on your way up to make the delivery or on your way back down to the front desk?"

"I passed by lots of people, but I thought they were just regular guests."

Spinelli pulled his wallet from his pocket, flipped it open, and retrieved a photo of him and Shannon. He stared at the photo for a brief moment wondering where he'd gone wrong. In the picture he was dressed as Santa, and Shannon wore a little red velvet dress.

The photo had been taken two months earlier while they were working in the Santa display at the mall. This was when he'd first met her. He remembered feeling utterly ridiculous through the whole undercover Santa job, but he did it for her. And it was a good thing he did or she probably wouldn't be here today to tell her story. He'd snatched her from the boney hands of the Grim Reaper and took a bullet in the process. His chest tightened at the awful memory and what followed. He shook his head. So this is how she repaid him. She kissed another man; a man who had just turned up dead.

He tore his gaze from the photo and handed it to Ashley, "Have you ever seen this woman?" He watched as Walker glanced at the photo then shifted his confused gaze to him. He knew Walker wanted to say something, but he held his tongue.

"Yes," Ashley replied with a nod.

Spinelli's heart leaped into his throat. His lungs drained. Blood rushed through his veins at the speed of light. His mind reeled for a response. He hoped his ears had deceived him. "She was here?" he asked. His voice cracked.

"No, not here, but I've seen her before. That's Ms. O'Hara. She's my family's caseworker. My stepdad, he's a real prick to my mom and my younger stepbrothers," Ashley's eyes filled with tears again. "Oh no, is she okay? She's been a godsend to my mother."

Spinelli's throat cleared and his lungs inflated. "She's fine." Ashley's questioning gaze stayed on him but he offered nothing more.

He refused to look at Walker who'd surely want an explanation. He'd get one as soon as they were finished at the crime scene.

Spinelli and Walker milled around the crime scene with a couple of forensic officers. Nothing looked unusual.

They headed toward the elevator. Walker pressed the button. They waited. Spinelli could feel Walker's curious gaze on him. The doors opened, they stepped in, and the doors closed. They were alone.

"Okay, do you want to tell me what in the hell that was all about?"

Spinelli looked at Walker, the elevator stopped, and a woman and child stepped through the doors. They rode the elevator in silence, and all exited on the main floor. Once in the unmarked, Spinelli spilled his guts. "The vic, Dr. Joshua Meyers, is the man I saw Shannon kissing in the hallway."

Walker's silence about killed Spinelli, and again Walker stared back with the usual unemotional look on his face. He started the car but didn't shift it into drive. "Where is she now? Where was she going when she left us in the precinct?"

"Church. You can't possibly…there's got be a reasonable explanation for this," Spinelli squeaked out.

"Don't get me wrong. There's no way she killed him or anyone else for that matter. But the way it looks right now, she was one of the last people to see the victim alive. I have to wonder, is she in danger as well? I know she doesn't fit the profile of the other vics. All that said, I am puzzled by the fact you saw her…," his voice trailed off.

Spinelli swallowed hard and finished Walker's sentence. "Kissing him. I know what I saw."

"So, where is she?"

"She's at St. Mary's church helping with the fundraiser."

"What kind of fundraiser?"

Spinelli thought for a moment. His pulse pounded in his ears. His mouth went dry. "She's playing the role as cupid's helper," his voice almost a whisper.

Walker's eyes widened. "What?"

"They're performing singing valentines and delivering chocolates and flowers."

Walker shifted the car into gear, pulled into traffic, and headed in the direction of St. Mary's.

Spinelli pulled his cell phone out and tapped the display screen. A picture of Shannon loaded. Her bright emerald eyes stared back at him. He pulled her up on the contact list and put the phone to his ear. The call went to voicemail. "Damn it!" he growled.

"What's the matter?" Walker asked.

"She's not answering."

"Could be by design."

"That's not funny. I expect that kind of comment from Marsh. Not you," Spinelli snapped.

Walker flashed his eyes in Spinelli's direction. "It wasn't meant to be funny. I was just trying to say that maybe she's busy, and everything is okay."

"Oh."

Within minutes Walker had parked the unmarked in the church's parking lot. A single exterior light shined above the side door facing the street. They sprang out of the car and rushed to that door assuming it would be unlocked. They were right. Just inside the doorway was a lit stairwell leading to the basement. Following the scent of roses, they raced down the stairs to find the priest and a couple of what he assumed to be "Sisters" indulging in some Valentine's Day chocolates. It was much easier to identify nuns in the old days when they wore habits.

Spinelli flashed his badge and introduced himself and Walker. Wide smiles instantaneously stretched across the faces of the priest and women. "So, you're Shannon's beau," one of the ladies commented as she kept an inquisitive eye on him. "I'm Sister Pat," then she gestured toward the other woman and the priest. "This is Sister Lora and Father Daniel."

He couldn't help but smile. They all looked so pleased; little did they know. "Yes, ma'am I am Shannon's boyfriend. Do you know where I can find her right now?"

Sister Pat lifted the reading glasses that hung by a chain around her neck and perched them on the end of her nose before she picked up the clipboard that lay on the table in front of her. "Oh, dear, they all had so many deliveries scheduled, and that poor girl has to do hers by herself since her partner didn't show up. We can try her cell phone to find out where she's at."

"She's by herself?"

Sister Pat fixed her soothing blue-eyed gaze on him, obviously picking up on his discontent. "Yes, we didn't have anyone else to send with her when she left. Father Daniel and Sister Lora just got back from their deliveries, and I was the only one left here to man the fort. Because she was alone, we sent her on the downtown business deliveries. You know, to the ladies and gentleman who are working tonight. The majority of them are working at stores or restaurants," Sister Pat paused and smiled. "People just love to surprise their loved ones at work."

Spinelli worked to get his voice in check. He knew he needed to get it together. "Can you tell me who she was supposed to work with tonight?"

"Joshua Meyers, but he didn't show up. That's so unlike him. I hope nothing happened to him."

Walker shot Spinelli a sideways glance. He knew what he needed to do. He didn't like it one bit, but he knew.

Spinelli shifted his gaze to Father Daniel. "Father, were you dressed like cupid earlier?"

"Yes."

"Can I borrow your costume?"

Father hesitated for a moment. He must have read the concerned look in Spinelli's eyes. "Sure." He glanced toward Sister Pat. "Why don't you call Shannon and see if you can locate her. Maybe Mr. Spinelli can catch up with her and help her finish with her deliveries."

Sister Pat nodded and picked up the phone receiver. Spinelli leaned toward her. "I'd like to surprise her if I could."

She nodded before her call connected. "Hi, Shannon. This is Sister Pat. We received two more delivery requests in your area. Do you think you could take them on and still finish by 8:00 or so?...Uh huh...oh no, dear, we'll have someone meet you at your next stop with the names, addresses, flowers, and candy. Where is your next stop and when do you think you'll be there?...Okay, got it."

Sister Pat hung up the phone receiver and fixed her gaze on Spinelli. "She's working North Water Street right now, and she's just about to stop at a client's, so that will take some time. Her next stop is at Billy's

BBQ. She's delivering to a waitress there. She'll be there in about twenty minutes."

"Okay, we'll meet her there. Sister, do your delivery teams check in with you through the course of the night or do they just make all their deliveries and check back with you when they're done."

"Unless there is some sort of issue, we don't hear from them."

"How many teams do you have working tonight?" Spinelli asked as he wondered how many more potential dead cupid candidates there were out on the loose.

"There were twelve delivery teams counting Shannon's."

Shannon was working alone, and Father Daniel was back already, so that only left ten of their cupids, plus now himself, roaming the streets.

Father handed Spinelli his cupid costume. It hung from a hanger, wings, and all.

Spinelli stared at his ridiculous reflection in the bathroom mirror. He couldn't help but wonder how he came to be here; in a church of all places, wearing a white toga. He slipped his arms through the wing straps. He shook his head. He must be crazy.

His mind drifted to thoughts of Shannon. Two months ago she had him parading around as Santa Claus, and now here he stood, dressed as the god of love, or desire, depending upon whose perspective you're using. He looked down at the bow and quiver of golden arrows leaning against the wall. *Golden arrows. True love. Yeah, right. Maybe I should be a womanizer like Marsh and carry lead arrows for erotic love. Obtaining that is more realistic!* He thought that maybe he should pinch himself. Perhaps this was just a nightmare. No such luck. He grabbed the bow and quiver and headed out of the restroom.

The second he stepped out of the bathroom he caught Walker's amused gaze. If the circumstances were different and they weren't chasing after a killer, Spinelli was sure Walker would have met him with full-blown laughter.

Sister Pat handed Walker two bouquets of roses, two heart shaped boxes of candy, and a piece of paper containing the addresses of the additional deliveries they needed to make. She studied Spinelli with a look of amusement in her eyes. "Well, you should be all set. Shannon will be waiting for you."

Chapter Nine

Walker parked the police car a few stalls up and on the opposite side of the street from Billy's BBQ. They waited for Shannon to arrive. She pulled up in her blue Chevy Impala within a few minutes and parked in front of the restaurant.

Spinelli flung his car door open and attempted to slide out, but his wing got tangled up with the seatbelt and jerked him back into the seat. He fumbled with the shoulder strap and wing. "Damn it," he growled. His patience was shot.

By the time he finally freed himself, Shannon was standing at his side. The look on her face was unmistakable. She was pissed. He supposed she was upset because of how he treated her earlier in the office. A tinge of guilt rippled through him but was quickly pushed aside by hurt and anger as memories of why he treated her poorly in the first place flashed through his mind. The infamous Dr. Joshua Meyers. The now dead Dr. Meyers.

Spinelli met her gaze. The intense look in her eyes pinned him to the car as if he were a humongous magnet. Her nostrils flared. He was glad her hands were full of flowers and candy. He feared she might smack him if they were free. She unclenched her jaw. "What are you doing here, and why are you dressed as cupid?"

"I...I'm here to help you with your deliveries," Spinelli stammered. She had a way of making him falter when they'd first met, back when he wasn't on her 'favorite' person list, but he thought he'd gotten beyond that. The lead weight on his tongue told him otherwise.

"Why?"

Because your secret lover has been murdered, and you're a suspect. "I want to spend some time with you on Valentine's Day."

Shannon bent over and looked around Spinelli. Her eyes seemed to soften. "Hi, Brad."

"Hi, Shannon," Walker replied from the driver's seat.

"Work pulled you away from your Valentine's Day plans as well, I take it?"

Walker nodded. "Well, you know how it is."

"I'm sorry. I'm sure Jeana understands."

"You know, Shannon, if you take this ornery cuss off my hands, I might still be able to resurrect some of the evening with Jeana."

Shannon shot Spinelli a sideways glare then glanced back at Walker. "For you, Brad, I'll do it, but only for you," she reiterated as she shifted her icy cold glare back to Spinelli.

Spinelli leaned into the backseat and grabbed the flowers and candy Sister Pat had given him for the extra deliveries. He slid them into Shannon's car. He watched as Walker pulled away from the curb. He knew Walker wasn't going too far, just out of Shannon's view. He'd be listening on his earpiece.

Shannon nodded toward Billy's BBQ, though she didn't have to. A blind man could have found his way just by following the wonderful aroma of deep fried food. The smell made Spinelli's mouth water. His stomach growled. He realized he hadn't eaten anything all day. He'd been called out of bed early by Captain Jackson to attend to the murder of Mike Carter, their first cupid. Then when he went to ask Shannon out for lunch, he caught her kissing Dr. Meyers, and before he could even return to the precinct he'd gotten the call to investigate the murder Chad Williams, the third cupid. And now instead of sitting down to dinner, he found himself delivering flowers and candy to starry-eyed victims of love.

"We're delivering to a waitress by the name of Stacey Hicks. What are you going to sing to her?" Shannon asked.

"What?"

"That's what I'm asking you. What are you going to sing to her? You're cupid. It's your job."

The shrillness in her voice sent a shiver up his spine. It was going to be a long couple of hours. Evidently he hadn't thought this whole cupid thing all the way through. He couldn't sing, and he certainly didn't know any cutesy love songs. And even if he did know any, he certainly wasn't in the mood to sing to any poor love-struck saps.

He could tell by the look in her eyes she was serious, and she'd make his life even more miserable if he didn't do it. Additionally, she didn't think he could do it. He'd show her. He thought for a moment. There must be some half-assed love song he could sing. All that came to mind was Adam Sandler singing the song "Love Stinks" in the movie *The Wedding Singer*. That certainly wasn't going to work.

His mouth went dry. Sweat beaded on his temples. *Christ almighty, its twenty-five degrees outside, and I'm sweating. Freaking women. I didn't sign up for this!*

It took a moment, but a song came to him. He'd heard on a car commercial some time ago.

Spinelli gestured toward the front door of the restaurant. "After you, my dear."

Shannon stomped off toward the door. If her heels hit the pavement any harder, they'd crack the sidewalk. She pushed through the door letting it fall shut behind her. Spinelli grabbed the handle and passed through as well.

All heads turned toward them. He felt like such an idiot; dressed in a white toga, holding a fake gold colored bow, almost child sized, with a quiver full of golden arrows slung over his shoulder. People smiled in their direction. Spinelli fought the urge to roll his eyes. *Fools, blinded by the hype of the holiday.*

He listened as Shannon spoke with the hostess. Her voice was soft and sweet. He remembered when she talked to him like that. It was just this morning. *All a front. A big fat lie.*

The hostess motioned to a waitress, catching her attention almost immediately. Her nametag said Stacey. The hostess waved her over. All eyes followed the young woman who stepped in their direction with a degree of hesitation. "Can I help you?" she asked.

Shannon smiled softly at her. "Dustin sent us," she said as she reached over and took the bouquet of roses from Spinelli and handed them to Stacey. Spinelli still held the heart shaped box of chocolates in his hand. He didn't want to let them go. He needed something to occupy his shaky fingers. He glanced around the room. All eyes were still on them. His heart thudded in his chest.

Shannon stepped back. Her smile grew wider. She gestured toward Spinelli. "Dustin also sent a message for you from Cupid."

Spinelli's cheeks burned. His pulse pounded. Maybe his head would explode, and he'd get out of this awful mess. His mind raced to place the words of the song from the car commercial into order. It was a Nissan commercial. No, it was Honda. *For crissake sake, who in the hell cares what kind of commercial it was? Just sing the stupid song already.* All eyes were still on him. He cleared his throat and broke out into a rendition of "You Are My Sunshine."

He kept his eyes on Stacey as he sang the short verse and swayed back and forth with both his shaky hands fixed to the box of chocolates. It was almost as if he was dancing with the box. A bright shade of red consumed her cheeks. Was he that bad? Her lips quivered but eventually broke into a full smile.

When he finished his song and dance, he handed her the chocolates as the crowd applauded.

Spinelli shifted his gaze to Shannon. She seemed surprised. She smiled and clapped as well. He imagined Walker listening to the whole ordeal though his earpiece. He imagined he'd never hear the end of it once the entire precinct found out. He took a bow, spun on his heel, and headed out the door.

He didn't have to turn around to know Shannon followed close behind him. The sound of her heels pounding against the cement assured him. Her steps didn't sound as heavy as when they first went into the restaurant. Maybe she was lightening up a bit. Wait a minute, why did he care if she was still mad? He was the one who was supposed to be pissed as hell. She's so damn beautiful, he'd almost forgotten.

Spinelli stomped toward Shannon's car without looking back at her. The automatic locks clicked, and he slid into the passenger seat. He didn't even attempt to open her door for her, even though he always opened her door. Shannon slid into the driver's seat and cranked the engine. Without a word she shifted the car into drive and pulled into traffic. Spinelli checked the side mirror. Walker followed close behind.

Shannon plucked the clipboard from between the seats and handed it to him. He glanced at the list of deliveries. The next one was only four blocks away. He read the name aloud, "Bernard Mathison." A guy? How in the hell was he going to keep a straight face singing a love song to a guy?

"Yep, his wife calls him Bernie." He shot Shannon a sideways glance. The corner of her mouth twitched as if she were trying to suppress an unstoppable smile. He was sure she was enjoying his severe discomfort.

Shannon parked the car on the same side of the street as Bernie's bar. Spinelli's mind raced for a song. He couldn't possibly sing "You Are My Sunshine" to a guy. It just wouldn't be right, and the only song filtering through his brain at present was Bon Jovi's "You Give Love a Bad Name." So not appropriate. True maybe, but not appropriate.

Spinelli climbed out of the car and took the box of chocolates from Shannon. He needed something to occupy his hands. Shannon pushed her way through the large glass door and stepped into Bernie's bar. The room was long and narrow. All heads turned in their direction as the bells on the door clinked. Nearly every barstool was occupied at the old worn wooden bar, which ran almost the entire length of the room. A few patrons sat at the small tables lining the opposite wall of the bar. The middle of the room was home to two pool tables, neither being used at the moment.

Shannon stepped toward the opening at the end of the bar. She handed the bartender the bouquet of roses and leaned toward the large burly man and kissed him on the cheek. He smiled and winked at her. His bright blue eyes twinkled. His curly red hair matched Shannon's. Who was this guy, and how did she know him?

"Hi, Uncle Bernie."

"Hi, sweetie. I see your Aunt Maggie is up to her little games again," he said as he shifted his gaze from Shannon to Spinelli and looked him over.

Her uncle, other than the bright red hair, looked nothing like her or any of her immediate family whom he'd only seen in pictures.

Shannon motioned to him, and he stepped closer to them. All eyes still on him. The scent of stale cigars and beer penetrated his nostrils.

"Well, son, what delightful song has my darling picked out for me this year?"

He could see the snickers down the bar. This lumberjack was really going to make him sing to him. Shannon's challenging gaze was just the incentive he needed. He eyed Bernie. He looked like he might have a sense of humor. Spinelli cleared his throat and broke out into a loud rendition of Bon Jovi's "You Give Love a Bad Name." He was loud, animated, short and sweet about it, and when he finished chuckles broke out down the bar.

"Sounds like Maggie's got your number, Bernie," someone yelled from several stools down. More laughter followed. Bernie laughed as well.

"You kids got time for a lightning fast one?"

Shannon shook her head. "We can't stay. We have a few more deliveries."

He stepped forward and gave Shannon a hug then he reached over and extended his hand to Spinelli. "Nicely done, son, but a bit of advice. Don't quit your day job." Bernie roared with laughter. Shannon's sweet giggle echoed in Spinelli's ears as well.

She gestured toward him. "Uncle Bernie, this is Nick Spinelli."

Bernie's smile widened. "So you're the young lad who's captured the heart of our little Shannon."

Out of the corner of his eye he could see Shannon's cheeks turn as red as her dress.

Bernie obviously didn't have a clue about his dear little Shannon.

"I can't believe you kids are running around dressed like you are tonight with all that's gone on today," Bernie whispered as he leaned toward Spinelli. "Are you undercover again, just like you were with the Santa and Elf case at Christmas?"

Spinelli looked beyond Bernie. His clientele seemed to have gone about their business and paid no attention to Bernie's question. He could feel Shannon's sharp gaze burning a hole through him. How was he going to explain this and the fact her fiancé was dead, and she was a suspect? Guilt consumed him. He hadn't decided when he was going to tell her about Dr. Joshua, but it looked as though the time was drawing near.

"What's he talking about, Nick?" Shannon asked. Her voice squeaked.

He knew he needed to look at her, but he just couldn't bring himself to do so. She tugged at his arm. "What's going on?"

He shifted his gaze to her. Her eyes pleaded with him. "We'll talk about it in the car."

Chapter Ten

Spinelli held his hand out. Shannon dropped her car keys into it. He opened the passenger door to her vehicle, and she slid in. He climbed in on the driver's side.

He'd hardly shut the door before she began questioning him. "What was Uncle Bernie talking about? Are you undercover?"

Spinelli started the car and flipped on the heater. He wasn't sure why he turned it on, the heat emitting from his pores was surely enough to heat the car. He cleared his throat and expelled a breath. "I think Bernie was probably referring to the cupids that were murdered today. It was all over the news. Didn't you hear about it?" he asked trying to keep it light.

"When would I have had time to watch the news? I worked all day then I went to the church to help with the fundraiser, and I've been making deliveries until now," Shannon snapped.

"So you worked all day?"

"Yes."

"You didn't leave your office at all during the day?" Spinelli questioned before considering the consequences.

Shannon's eyes watered and her lips quivered. Did she know why he was questioning her? It certainly didn't look good that she knew one of the dead cupids and that he had seen them leaving the government building together just hours before the body was found. That coupled with the fact that Bethany put his time of death at around 2:00 p.m. didn't help matters either.

Spinelli thought about their first victim who'd been found at 3:45

a.m. Bethany had placed his time of death at shortly after midnight. Could Shannon have had anything to do with the death of Mike Carter? Spinelli's chest tightened. He had arrived home at about that same time, midnight, to find Shannon sleeping in his bed. He hadn't been surprised to find her there since they'd spent nearly every night together since they'd started dating. He'd gotten home so late because he, Walker, and Marsh were held up at the precinct closing a case. He wondered what time she'd arrived at his house. He hadn't given it any consideration earlier, but a shadow of doubt now hovered over him. Exactly what time did she arrive at his house? Where was she prior to that?

A vision of Tony Rosso's dead body surfaced in Spinelli's head. Tony had been found at 8:00 a.m. Bethany estimated his time of death at about 4:00 a.m. *Hah! Shannon was in my bed at 4:00 a.m.!* He could verify she'd been in his bed since at least midnight. There was no way she had anything to do with Rosso's death. Spinelli's mind spun. *What in the hell am I thinking? Get it together. This is Shannon. Sweet, innocent Shannon. Good God, how am I going to tell her Joshua Meyers is dead? Was he really her fiancé?* Shannon's nostrils flared. "Nick, why are you grilling me? Why are you really here? And why were you such a jerk to me earlier today?"

He stared into her furious eyes, debating his response. He glanced into the backseat to find the flowers and candy they'd yet to deliver. She'd never be able to finish the deliveries if he told her now of the death of Joshua Meyers or if he confronted her about witnessing their kiss.

"Fine. Do what you always do. Clam up. If we don't talk about it, it will just go away, and you won't have to deal with it," Shannon snapped as she shifted her body and stared out the front windshield. She clicked on her seat belt and crossed her arms over her chest.

Spinelli grabbed the clipboard where he'd fastened the paper containing the additional addresses Sister Pat had given him. The next delivery was several blocks away at another restaurant. He hoped there wouldn't be as many patrons in this restaurant as there were in Billy's BBQ. He was so embarrassed singing in front of all of them. He wasn't in the mood for singing love songs when this whole escapade started, let alone now.

He parked in the parking lot next to the restaurant and had hardly cut the engine before Shannon bolted from the car. Spinelli grabbed the flowers and chocolates from the backseat and in a couple of quick steps was on her heels. She stepped up to the hostess station and asked for Naomi. Her tone was soft and sweet, far different from the last time she'd spoken.

He went through his routine. He'd never get used to this. Only one more to go then he could get on with dealing with Shannon and Dr. Joshua Meyers.

They climbed back into the car. Shannon's smile had disappeared along with the warmness in her eyes. Spinelli grabbed the clipboard from between the seats. He couldn't help but chuckle.

Shannon's cold eyes cut to him. "What's so funny?" she asked in a tone sharper than a samurai sword.

Spinelli's throat constricted choking off his chuckle.

He swallowed the lump in his throat. "The next stop is at Madam Layla's Lingerie Shop."

Shannon shook her head and shifted her eyes forward.

Spinelli pressed the accelerator to the floor. He wanted to get this over with.

He parked on the street in front of the store. Through the plate glass window he could see several customers milling about. Both men and women shuffled through the racks of lingerie. Last minute shoppers he supposed.

Shannon opened the door and sprang out like a jack-in-the-box on speed. Evidently she wanted to get this over with as well.

He followed her into the shop and zoned in on the older woman behind the counter. He assumed her to be Madam Layla.

He figured her to be in her early sixties. She stepped around the counter to help a young gentleman with his lingerie choice. Her leopard patterned leggings and matching five-inch spike heels caught his attention. She looked like an ex-Las Vegas dancer with her long thin frame, tall flowing hair, and heavily painted face. Her tight black sweater clung to her large breasts and small waist.

When she finished ringing up the young man's purchase, they approached her. She raked over Spinelli, not just once, but twice. "What can I do for you?" she asked, keeping her gaze fixed firmly on him as if Shannon weren't even there.

Shannon cleared her throat drawing Madam Layla's attention. "We've been sent here by Harold."

The woman let out a girlish giggle. "That sweet man. Will he ever give up?" she asked as her eyes floated back to Spinelli.

He handed the bouquet of roses to her. She leaned over the counter and took them from him as she eyed the entire length of him. He broke into what had become his routine. He wasn't even nervous this time, of course the store wasn't nearly as occupied as the restaurants and bar had been.

During his entire performance, Layla's seducing eyes never left him. When he finished, he handed her the box of chocolates. She reached forward and snatched the chocolates with one hand and set them on the counter. With her other hand, she latched onto his wrist. "I've got something for you," she glanced at Shannon, "and for your cute little friend, too."

Layla kept her grip on him and pulled him along. Shannon hesitated but followed.

She led them to the back of the store and sifted through a few garments hanging on a clothing rack. "Ah ha, here they are. These would be perfect for such a nice looking young couple."

Spinelli instantly hardened at the vision of Shannon wearing the skimpy garment Layla held high in the air. He could easily see the hot pink lingerie contrasting against Shannon's milky white skin, and her small, pale, round breasts partially exposed over the top of the low-cut fur-lined bodice. He imagined the smooth feel of the fabric under his fingertips. He pictured himself plunging his hand between the silky material and her soft smooth skin. His groin tightened with need.

Layla's other hand held a hanger with a pair of silky red boxer shorts. Large, hot-pink, heart-shaped buttons held the fly shut. Hearts, the same color and size, lined the waistband. He wouldn't be caught dead wearing those. He reconsidered. Perhaps if Shannon agreed to her garment, he'd agree to his. The vision of her wearing the lingerie with a pair of thigh-high fishnet stockings and spiked heels would likely make him agree to anything, especially if she were to add a set of wrist cuffs and a rose tipped whip like the ones he saw on the shelf near the checkout counter.

Layla glanced about the store. "Hmm," she flipped her long poufy hair over her shoulder and then fixed her eyes on Shannon. "You know, dear, I've got the perfect accessories over here to go with these," she said as she motioned for them to follow her.

Shannon hesitated and stepped back. Her normally pale cheeks were as red as the boxer shorts Layla held in her hand.

"Oh, sweetie, you need to loosen up a bit and have some fun," Layla said as she shifted her gaze to Spinelli and winked, "and I bet this handsome fella here would be more than willing to help you along with that." She undressed him with her eyes again, "If I were thirty years younger, I would be giving him an open invitation before someone else did."

Spinelli took the garments from Layla's hands. "We'll take these. What else is it you want to show us?"

He didn't need to look at Shannon to know her disapproving gaze was on him. He welcomed her discomfort, just as she welcomed his during the whole singing cupid thing.

He followed Layla to the display he'd seen earlier, the one that held the wrist cuffs and whips. It was as if Layla could read his mind. She snatched them off the shelf and set them on the checkout counter.

Spinelli reached into the small makeshift pocket sewn into the inside of his toga costume. It was barely large enough to hold is badge, ID, two bills and a credit card, but he was thankful it was there so he didn't have to wear his badge around his neck during this cupid escapade.

His groin had nearly made him forget he was angry with Shannon and that they still needed to resolve the Dr. Joshua issue. But he was too far into the purchase to turn back now, so he slapped his credit card on the counter. He knew Shannon was glaring at him, but he couldn't bring himself to return her gaze. She sighed heavily.

Madam Layla bagged the items and handed the bag to Spinelli. She flashed him a wink. "You kids have a nice Valentine's night."

"You, too."

Spinelli spun on his heel and headed out the door. Shannon huffed behind him. If she wasn't pissed enough before, she was surely pissed enough now.

By the time he'd tossed the lingerie bag into the back seat, Shannon had already slid into the passenger seat. Spinelli climbed into the driver's seat and cranked the engine. The smoke billowing from her ears made it difficult for him to see out the windshield.

Spinelli signaled and pulled into traffic. He drove fast. He glanced at the clock on the dashboard. He pressed the accelerator closer to the floorboard shooting over State Street; the street he should have turned on in order to head back to the precinct.

Shannon fixed her confused gaze on him. "Where are we going? We're done with the deliveries. Isn't your truck at the precinct?"

"Yeah, it is. But I have one quick stop to make yet."

"Where?"

Spinelli's cheeks heated. He'd wanted to make this particular stop earlier in the evening, when he was by himself, but time just didn't allow for it.

* * * *

The car shot over Juneau Street before Shannon realized where they might be heading. Was he really going to the foster home of the Washington kids?

The Washington home was the first home she and Spinelli had visited when he'd been assigned to help in the Social Services Department. At that time, the Washington kids lived with their parents in a dilapidated apartment building on Cherry Street, a gang infested area. Not only was their dad a drug dealer, he was also physically abusive to their mom. And though he beat her, she'd refused to leave him because she needed to keep close ties with her cocaine dealer. As a result, Shannon and Spinelli removed the kids from the home on that particular day and brought them to their new foster home where they've lived ever since.

Shannon recalled Spinelli's evident apprehension during the entire process. Certainly, nobody is happy or comfortable when removing children from the home of their parents, but Spinelli's anguish during the whole ordeal was like none she'd ever seen before on such a call. She'd later found out that Cherry Street was the very same street where he grew up; in an environment not so different from the Washington kids.

A few days after the kids were placed in foster care, the foster mom had brought them to the mall to visit Santa. Spinelli just so happened to be playing Santa that day because he was working his undercover assignment. Somewhere during this chain of events, Spinelli and the eldest of the Washington kids, Lesha, age seven, had developed some sort of bond.

Spinelli pulled up to the curb of the foster home and cut the engine.

Shannon glanced at her watch. "It's kind of late. The kids might be sleeping."

He shook his head. "Nope. Sandi knew I was coming, so she was going to keep them up. I texted her earlier."

He texted her?

They slid out of the car and walked up to the front door of the older well-kept, two-story home. It was a nice, clean home; far different from what the Washington kids had previously been accustomed. And as for Sandi, Shannon really liked her. She was a loving and caring woman. She and her husband Al, both in their mid-forties, never had kids of their own, but they saw to the needs of many foster kids through the years.

Spinelli knocked on the door. Al answered and gestured for them to enter as he eyed Spinelli who still wore his cupid costume.

"It's a long story," Spinelli said before Al even said a word.

They walked through the small entryway, and the second they entered the living room, the kids' eyes lit up at the sight of Spinelli. Sandi smiled in his direction.

Lesha jumped off the couch and ran up to Spinelli with her arms open. He scooped her up and gave her a hug. She kissed him on the cheek before he set her back down. Lesha's brother, Darius, age three, kept his distance. Samuel, a foster child from a different home, who'd been with Sandi for some time now stood next to Darius. Christina, the youngest of the Washington children at eleven months, was nowhere to be seen. Shannon assumed she was already in bed.

Shannon watched and listened as Spinelli interacted with the children. Her first impression of him, when she'd met him a little over two months ago, was so incredibly wrong. At that time, he'd seemed cold and harsh to people, especially children. But it didn't take her long to realize that was just his exterior layer. His warm and caring interior layers, hidden firmly beneath the surface, didn't take long to emerge once the outer tier had been penetrated.

Spinelli handed each of the children a valentine and one to Sandi, with Christina's name printed on the envelope. Shannon recalled seeing the envelopes lying on the back seat of her car earlier but hadn't really given any thought as to whom they were for.

Judging from Lesha's smile that stretched from ear to ear, she'd realized her valentine included a trip to Chuck E. Cheese. She looked at Darius' and Samuel's valentines and then explained to them what those certificates meant. Their eyes lit up, Samuel's a bit more than Darius'. At just three years old, Darius always seemed leery. Shannon hoped he'd shake it someday and enjoy a carefree childhood.

"Do you guys have something to say to Mr. Spinelli before you go to bed?" Sandi asked as she glanced at each one of the children.

Each child, in turn, thanked Nick.

Sandi flashed a warm smile as well. "Thank you, Nick. The children always enjoy seeing you." She shifted her gaze to Shannon. "It's nice to see you, too."

Shannon returned her smile then glanced at Spinelli. His normal olive colored skin tone looked red. Was he blushing? She thought about Sandi's words. *The children always enjoy seeing you. How often does he stop here? And when?*

She wondered how she got so lucky; the man's heart was truly made of gold. Her heart ached at the thought of what happened today with her and Joshua. She truly didn't mean to kiss him. She desperately needed to fix this with Nick. She had to make him understand and forgive her.

Spinelli cleared his throat. "I'm sorry for getting here so late. We'll get out of here so you can get them to bed." He shifted his gaze to the kids. "You guys be good now, okay?"

The kids nodded.

* * * *

Spinelli opened the car door for Shannon, and she slid into the passenger seat. He hustled around to the driver's side and climbed into the car. Though the temperature hovered around twenty-five degrees outside, he was sure the thermometer would read in the teens if he wasn't so warm. The whole while they were in the foster home, he could feel

Shannon's heated gaze on him. He knew he'd have some explaining to do. She wouldn't be able to just let this go and not grill him about why they stopped there or why he stops there regularly.

He wondered why himself. He'd been visiting them once a week since the foster mom had taken the kids to the mall to see him as Santa. The Christmas wish Lesha shared with him that day nearly broke his heart in half. He recalled how she climbed up onto his lap and whispered in her sweet little voice. *I would like a new mom and dad for me and my brother and sister, then maybe Darius wouldn't be scared and cry all the time. You know, maybe a mom like Ms. O'Hara or the new foster mom, one that would love us and take care of us.*

He hoped those kids would never have to go back to their parents. He'd give his right arm to make her wish come true. His chest tightened. He knew the truth. From his own past experience, he knew in all likelihood those kids would bounce between their parents and foster care more times than he'd care to know. Though he hated the flawed system, he figured it was better than no system at all.

"Nick, why didn't you tell me you visit the Washington kids?"

He stared out the windshield. *Why can't she ever just leave well enough alone? Why does she always have to talk about everything?* He shifted the car into gear. His mind raced for an answer. He knew he'd have to answer her. She'd hound him until he did. "I guess it just never came up." *Kind of like your little fiancé secret.*

Out of the corner of his eye he saw her shoulders stiffen. Her lips pulled into a thin line.

Evidently he hadn't kept the sharpness out of his tone as he'd planned.

A few beats passed before she sucked in a breath and expelled it. "It was very sweet, what you did for those kids tonight."

He shrugged.

She shifted in her seat. Her gaze fixed on him. His already hot cheeks were now flaming. *Why can't she ever just say her piece and leave it alone? All I did was bring them a gift. That's it, nothing else. End of story.*

Her lips parted. "Whether you believe it or not, those kids adore you, especially Lesha. Your actions have impacted those kids' lives more positively than anyone else has so far in their young lives."

What was she trying to do to him? He didn't need this kind of pressure. He just wanted to help a few kids who'd been dealt a shitty hand.

Chapter Eleven

Spinelli parked Shannon's car in the lot behind the building, next to his truck. She reached for her door handle, paused, and looked back at him. "Are you coming over tonight? I really need to talk to you, Nick."

He glanced at his watch. It was already after 8:30 p.m. So much for his Valentine's Day plans. A hint of sadness passed through her eyes at his hesitation.

"I can't. We're in the middle of something big here, and I really need you to come inside with me for a bit."

A look of fear trailed the curiosity that rushed through her eyes. She climbed out of the vehicle and kept pace at his side as they entered the precinct.

Marsh looked up from behind a table full of laptops as they approached him. He gave Spinelli a once over and roared with laughter. "Walker described it to me but I gotta tell you he didn't do it justice. Nice wings," Marsh's head bounced up and down like a bobble-head doll.

Spinelli wanted nothing more than to smack the smirk off his face. Before he could say anything, Walker's heels pounded against the wood floor in their direction. All eyes shifted to Walker.

Shannon raised an eyebrow. "Brad, I thought you were going home to spend time with Jeana."

Walker shifted his gaze to the floor. He looked like a puppy who'd been scolded for chewing on his master's shoes.

Shannon shifted her gaze to Spinelli. "What's going on here?"

"We need to talk, but first I need to get the hell out of this ridiculous outfit," Spinelli replied as he reached toward Walker for his clothes. He was glad Walker remembered to grab them from the backseat of their unmarked squad car.

Spinelli returned from the restroom a moment later. He now wore his usual attire; a pair of jeans and a long sleeved polo shirt. And most importantly, his shiny gold badge hung by a chain around his neck.

Shannon had taken a seat at the table across from Marsh. They were making small talk. The table abutted to Spinelli's desk. A red heart shaped box of chocolates sat on the center of his desk. It wasn't there when he had left earlier. He glanced at Marsh. "Where did that come from?"

Marsh shrugged. "I don't know."

Spinelli looked at Shannon. She shrugged as well. He could see the frustration in her eyes. He imagined she wanted to know what in the hell was going on.

He returned his gaze to Marsh. "You didn't see who put it there?"

"No, it isn't like I sat here and stared at your desk the entire time you were gone."

Spinelli thought about tearing into the chocolates. He hadn't eaten all day, and he was starving.

"Nick, it's getting late, and I'd like to go home soon. What is it you wanted to talk to me about?" Shannon asked, annoyance oozing through her words.

Walker and Marsh busied themselves. No moral support from them.

Spinelli plucked a photo of Dr. Joshua Meyers from a manila folder on his desk and held it up for Shannon to see. "Do you know this man?" Shannon leaned forward and glanced at the picture. She shifted her gaze to meet his. Her eyes watered, and she nodded. Spinelli wondered if her eyes watered because she'd been busted, or because she knew what had happened to Meyers today.

Spinelli lowered his shaky hand. His nerves were shot. "When was the last time you saw him?"

Shannon chewed on her bottom lip for a moment. She released it and blew out a sigh. "This afternoon. I last saw him this afternoon."

"What time?"

"I dropped him off at his hotel shortly before 2:00." Her confused gaze stayed on him.

He feared the answer to the next question, but he had to ask it anyhow. He knew she'd tell the truth. She was simply incapable of lying. "How do you know him?"

She shifted her gaze to the floor. "We were once engaged," she replied in a whisper. "But until today, I hadn't seen him for a couple of years."

Spinelli leaned forward. "Did you ever think to tell me you're engaged?"

"I'm not engaged now. I said I was once engaged," Shannon snapped back as she met his gaze again.

"That's not exactly how he put it."

Shannon shot him a frown. "What do you mean? When did you talk to Joshua?"

"I didn't talk to him. I heard him say it to you in the hall."

Her green-eyed gaze widened.

Spinelli leaned back in his chair and crossed his arms over his chest. "I believe the words I heard were 'Aren't you happy to see your fiancé?'"

"You heard that?"

Spinelli cocked his head to the side. "Yeah, do you want me to repeat what I saw right before I heard that, too?"

She lowered her gaze then looked up at him through her long lashes. "It's not what it looked like, and I tried to talk to you about it when I came down here earlier this afternoon but you blew me off and didn't give me a chance."

"What's to explain? Everything seemed pretty clear when his tongue was in your mouth."

Spinelli sprang to his feet and stepped back. He didn't like the intensity of the surge of jealousy flowing through his veins. He didn't like the fact that she could wind him up like this. A couple of months ago, his life was a lot less complicated. If only he could turn back the hands of time.

Shannon rose to her feet as well. "I can't believe you'd think I'd…" She glanced about the precinct. "Do we have to talk about this here?"

Her gaze shifted to the crime board to Spinelli's immediate left. She squinted. Her eyes went wide, and what little color she had in her pale cheeks disappeared. She was whiter than the toga he'd been wearing earlier.

Spinelli realized what she'd seen. Pictures of the dead cupids were on the board. Her gaze was fixed on Joshua. She gasped. Her lips quivered, and tears rolled down her cheeks. Spinelli quickly stepped around the desk and pulled her to him. He couldn't help himself. He hated it when she cried. He knew her knees were weak. He supported her in his arms where she always seemed to fit perfectly. After a moment, he urged her to sit.

Shannon sat quietly, staring forward, as if trying to gather her thoughts. She swiped her hands across her moist cheeks.

Walker appeared and handed her a box of tissues and a bottle of water. Marsh stood at his side. Spinelli sat at his desk.

Shannon looked up at Walker. "What happened to Joshua?"

Walker pulled up a chair. "We received a call today at about 4:00 p.m. in regard to the deceased. He checked in at the Hyatt and ordered room service. A hotel employee found him when she delivered his order. We have reason to believe he was poisoned."

Shannon threw her hand over her mouth. Her gaze stayed fixed on Walker. "Shannon, we know Dr. Meyers was upstairs with you at about 1:00 and that you left together. Where did you go when you left here?"

She shifted her gaze to Spinelli and lowered her hand. "I took him to the Hyatt. He had taken a cab directly here from the airport. He thought he'd just stay with me, but I told him he couldn't because…because I was seeing someone, so I dropped him off at the Hyatt."

"So you went right from here to the Hyatt and didn't stop anywhere else?" Walker asked drawing Shannon's gaze back to him.

Shannon shook her head.

"Where else did you stop?" Walker asked.

"I pulled into the parking lot up the street to talk to him for a minute."

Walker cocked a brow.

Shannon continued, "He made me so furious when he announced in front of everyone upstairs that we were engaged, I just needed to get him the hell out of here. I also wanted to take a minute to make him understand that we were through. Evidently, he didn't fully understand that when I gave the engagement ring back to him two years ago."

"So you talked for a couple of minutes and then took him to the Hyatt?"

Shannon nodded.

"What time was that?"

"We left here shortly after 1:00. I talked with him for five, maybe ten minutes before I drove him to the hotel."

Walker glanced at Spinelli then shifted his eyes back to Shannon. "Did you go up to his room?"

She looked at Spinelli and held his gaze for what seemed like an eternity. His thudding heart and pounding pulse was all he could hear. Both faded the longer he stared into her gaze, though he still wasn't sure he wanted to hear her answer. The ring in his pocket weighed down his twitching leg. The silence was excruciating. *Would she just answer already!*

She ripped her gaze from Spinelli's and returned it to Walker. "No, I didn't go to his room. We talked in the car for a bit, and then I left."

"Was he acting strange at all?"

Shannon thought for a moment. "No. He was a little upset, but he didn't act strange."

"Why was he upset?"

She looked at Spinelli. "I would imagine he didn't like that I declined his offer to go to his room, and that I reiterated the fact that I'm seeing someone else."

Walker nodded. "Where did you go after you dropped him off?"

"I stopped at Subway to pick up a sandwich, and then I came back to work."

"So you say you ended it and dropped him off at the hotel, and he was upset with you. Yet he agreed to work with you on the fundraiser tonight," Spinelli cut in.

Walker stepped back.

"He's an adult. He was doing what was best for the church," Shannon snapped back. Her condescending tone shamed him.

"I don't get it. Why would he want to help you with your church's fundraiser?"

"He went to my church. That's how I met him. In fact, the reason I haven't seen him for the past couple of years is because he was on a church mission trip in Nicaragua."

Spinelli caught Walker's sideways glance and snicker.

He felt like such an ass. The perfect Dr. Joshua Meyers was on a church mission trip. Reality check. He was jealous of a dead guy, and he knew if he didn't shut his mouth right here and now he'd be minus the woman he loved as well. But still, why did she kiss the wholesome doctor the way she did this afternoon?

"Nick, I don't want to discuss this now. Not here," Shannon said as her gaze drifted back to the crime board. He didn't really want to either, ever. He hated this type of confrontation in public or private.

Shannon squinted at the board again. "So, this is what Uncle Bernie was talking about?"

"Yes."

"How many cupids were murdered today?"

"Four so far."

"Four?"

"Yep."

Shannon leaned forward. Her mouth fell open. "Is that Mike…" her voice trailed off.

Spinelli, Walker, and Marsh fixed their gazes on her.

"You know Mike Carter?" Spinelli questioned.

Shannon's gaze shifted between the detectives. Several beats passed.

"Shannon, did you know Mr. Carter?" Walker asked in a tone a bit more controlled than the one Spinelli used seconds earlier.

She nodded.

"How did you know him?" Walker followed up.

She shifted her teary eyes to Spinelli. "We dated in high school," she whispered.

Spinelli looked at Walker and Marsh, "What in the hell?"

Walker stepped toward the crime board and pulled a photo of Tony Rosso, a clothed photo, not the one of him sprawled out on his boss' desk naked but for his wings. He held the photo up for Shannon to see. "Do you know who this is?" he asked.

Shannon nodded. "Tony Rosso."

"How did you know Mr. Rosso?" Walker asked.

This time she kept her gaze fixed on Walker. "My Uncle Bernie owns a bar downtown. Tony used to bartend for him. My uncle set us up, and we went out a few times."

Walker pulled another photo from the folder. "Do you know who this is?" he asked as he held the photo of the third cupid for her to see.

Tears rolled down her cheeks. She closed her eyes and sucked in a breath.

"Shannon?"

Her eyes fluttered open. "It's Chad Williams."

"Did you go out with him as well?" Walker asked.

She nodded and used the back of her hand to swipe the moisture from her cheeks.

Spinelli stood in disbelief.

Walker cleared his throat. "Let's take a step back here. In what order did you go out with these men?"

Shannon twisted off the top of the bottle of water Walker had given her earlier. She drank nearly half the bottle in one shot. She sucked in a deep breath and held it for a moment as if pausing to get her thoughts in order. She set the bottle on Spinelli's desk and expelled a breath. "I dated Mike Carter during the second half of my senior year in high school. I started dating Joshua in my senior year of college; he was already in medical school. We dated for a couple of years and got engaged. It seemed like the next step." She glanced at Spinelli. "Right before he left for Nicaragua I broke it off, but he obviously didn't take me seriously."

Shannon paused, closed her eyes, and sucked in a weighty breath.

She opened her eyes and continued. "After a while of not dating, everyone seems to want to set you up. Uncle Bernie set me up with Tony Rosso a few months after Joshua left. We only went out three or four times. Tony was nice enough but not my type. A few months or so after that a friend of mine set me up with Chad Williams. We only went out twice. I guess I wasn't his type."

"Were there any others?" Walker asked.

Shannon shifted her gaze to Spinelli then back to Walker. "Just Nick."

All eyes shifted to Spinelli.

"How ya feeling there, pal?" Marsh teased. He had no couth at times.

"Not funny! You're such an asshole!"

Silence filled the room. They all shifted their gazes back and forth.

Adrenaline rushed through Spinelli's veins. Was someone going to try to kill him today? Could he have been poisoned? Reality punched him in the gut, knocking the wind right out of him. Sweat beaded on his temples. His sweaty hands hadn't stopped shaking since he entered the precinct with Shannon. Was it just nerves or something more? His pulse pounded in his ears. Would this be the last time he'd hear his own pulse or the sweet sound of Shannon's soft feminine voice singing in his ears. He inhaled. The aroma of bitter coffee and stale pastries wafted through his nostrils but was quickly replaced by the pleasant refreshing scent of a fresh spring morning; Shannon's tantalizing scent. Would this be the last time he'd smell the confines of the precinct or her glorious heavenly scent? Would he ever get the opportunity to taste her sweet flavor again or feel her soft milky white skin under his fingertips? Confusion filled every cell in his body.

"Nick," Shannon whispered as she rose to her feet and stepped toward him.

He zoned in on her big green eyes. She looked concerned. He lifted his hand and stepped back. The hint of hurt that darkened her eyes pierced his heart.

He knew he needed to pull it together or else. He didn't want to think of the 'or else,' but it consumed his mind anyway.

Chapter Twelve

Spinelli and Walker questioned Shannon over and over in regard to who would possibly want to set her up. It didn't look good for her. In fact, if she hadn't spent the night at Spinelli's, she would have looked guilty as sin.

Bethany and Debra provided no news about the murders. All they'd confirmed thus far was that all four men had been poisoned with cyanide.

Spinelli's stomach growled reminding him and everyone else in a half-mile radius he hadn't eaten all day. He eyed the chocolates on his desk. No time now.

He looked over Marsh's shoulder as he sifted through the financial records of today's victims.

Walker was busy Googling cyanide. "I doubt you've been poisoned, Spinelli. It says here cyanide induces fatality in seconds following ingestion, especially on an empty stomach. On a full stomach it could take up to four hours. Good thing you haven't eaten all day. You never know what could be in your food."

Spinelli rolled his eyes. "Yeah, good thing. Where in the hell does someone get cyanide anyhow?"

Walker looked back at his computer screen. "It says here that after ingestion, certain chemicals can be changed by the body into cyanide. Products like old artificial nail polish remover or some chemicals found in old solvents and plastics manufacturing solutions contain such, but supposedly they've been removed from the market. Walker shook his head. "Who are we kidding? They probably got it right off of eBay in ready form."

"Is there anything there about quantity needed to ensure fatality?" Spinelli asked.

Walker nodded. "Yeah, but I don't know…well…it's hard to tell. I'm looking at some pathologist's blog, and he's got a bunch of mumbo jumbo on there about grams and milligrams and different kinds of cyanide. The only thing I can tell for sure is that if ingested, you'd better have your affairs in order."

"I think I may have found something here," Marsh interrupted as he pointed to some paperwork lying on his desk.

Spinelli leaned over his shoulder to get a better look. "What is it?"

"I had the IT Department print out Chad Williams' Internet records for the past week and there isn't much activity except for him logging onto the Wisconsin Department of Safety and Professional Services website. But on a couple of occasions he logged onto *backpage dot com*."

"So?"

"Well, the IT Department has a program that can track keystrokes, and they found this," he said as he pointed to a line in the middle of the text-filled page. "Judging from this, it looks like he logged into his hotmail account and answered a *backpage* ad for a male entertainer." Marsh slid his finger down to the next line of text. "It seems he planned to meet someone going by the name of Lady Lily. He agreed to meet her at the Morgan Bank building at 5:00 a.m. today."

Marsh paused and looked up at Spinelli and Walker. "The flower of death."

"Doesn't the orchid symbolize death?" Walker asked.

"No, I'm pretty sure it's the lily. I think I read that somewhere once."

The two debated the issue for a moment before Spinelli cut in, "For crissake, shut up about the damn flowers already." His gaze locked in on Marsh. "Have you found anything like this on Rosso's or Carter's computers?"

Marsh shook his head. "Not really, but just think about Rosso. According to his financial records, apartment, and the personal belongings we saw, he's living way beyond the means of a bartender. Maybe this guy was a male entertainer on the side, you know, maybe he's got himself a couple of rich, old, sugar mommas."

They stood in silence for a moment. Spinelli suspected Walker and Marsh were of like mind. It seemed to fit.

"And just look at Mike Carter's bank statement. The guy lost his job over six months ago and has been living with his sister since he ran out of cash. Then suddenly, bam, a $2,000 deposit was made into his bank account about a week ago. Maybe it was a payment for services rendered."

Walker shook his head. "I hear what you're saying, but this all seems just a bit far-fetched. How in the hell would someone be able to specifically contact four of Shannon's ex-boyfriends through a general ad on *backpage*? I mean, really, a shit-load of guys could have answered that ad. How would the killer even possibly begin to devise a way to reach these four specific guys? I've never been on *backpage* a day in my life. How would anyone know these guys would be?"

"I didn't get that far yet. I'm just saying we've got proof one of the vics answered an ad for a male entertainer, one of the vics was living a lifestyle above and beyond what his job could support, and one of the vics was unemployed and received an unaccounted for lump sum payment into his bank account," Marsh recapped.

"What about Meyers? He just got back into the country today," Walker commented.

"What, the Internet doesn't reach Nicaragua?" Marsh asked sarcastically.

Spinelli sighed. There were times he just wanted to smack the shit out of Marsh, and this was one of those times. He sucked in a deep breath to calm his temper. He thought for a moment. He massaged his pounding temples. On top of everything else, now he had a headache. "How could they possibly be connected?"

Walker and Marsh's eyes shifted to Shannon who sat silent, listening to their entire exchange.

Spinelli cocked his head to the side. "Other than the obvious. Maybe we need to talk to Sonny Tomes again. See if Carter and Williams frequented his bar."

Spinelli dialed Tomes' cell number. He answered on the third ring. Music blared in the background.

"Mr. Tomes?"

"Yes."

"This is Detective Spinelli. I take it you're at the bar?"

"Yep. Couldn't find anyone to fill in tonight for Tony."

"I see. So you're going to be there for a while?"

"Yep."

"We need to ask you a couple more questions. We'll be there shortly."

"Do what you gotta do. I'll be here."

Spinelli and Walker loaded into their unmarked. Shannon rode along as well. Spinelli wasn't about to let her out of his sight. Spinelli caught a glimpse of Shannon in the backseat. He'd debated sitting back there with her when they climbed into the car. Part of him wanted to hold her, comfort her. She looked confused and exhausted. He could tell by her silence that the day's events had taken their toll on her; she was rarely ever quiet. But another part of him was still angry with her, and this kept him at a distance. He still wanted an explanation as to why she'd kissed Meyers the way he'd seen her kissing him; all lips, teeth, and tongue. A friendly peck on the cheek he could have understood.

Walker parked on the street in front of Sonny's bar. All the bars and restaurants up and down the street looked busy. Full of patrons enjoying their Valentine's Day, Spinelli suspected.

They entered the establishment. It was busy. A wiry young man tended bar along with Sonny. He was tattooed and pierced. Looks wise, he couldn't be more opposite of Tony Rosso.

Sonny waved them over to the far end of the long worn wooden bar. There were fewer patrons at that end.

Spinelli pulled a photo of Mike Carter from the manila folder he carried and handed it to Sonny. "Do you know this guy?"

Sonny nodded. "Yep, he comes in pretty regularly. Never stays very long though."

"Did he and Tony know each other?"

"Yeah. He's been in while Tony was working. I don't know that they were buddies or anything, but I would imagine Tony talked to him like any other customer."

Spinelli set that photo down, grabbed one of Chad Williams, and handed it to Sonny. "Do you know this guy?"

Sonny nodded. "Yep. He comes in for lunch a couple times a week."

"I take it Tony knew him as well."

"Yeah. Hang on a second," Sonny added as he took a few steps toward the middle of the bar and tapped a beer for a young woman who'd set her empty mug up on the counter.

Spinelli glanced about the bar. An older woman sat to his left. One empty barstool separated them. She looked like a typical barfly. He figured her to be in her early sixties. Her dark copper hair was accented with a streak of blue in the bangs. Her makeup was painted on thick. She wore a tight red sweater and leaned forward with her boobs propped up on the bar. Maybe at her age, and considering the size of them, she didn't have the strength to hold them up on her own for too long a period of time.

She turned her head, checked out Spinelli, smiled, and leaned toward him. "I couldn't help but notice your photos. I've seen them both in here. They worked for Tony, you know." Her harsh, smoker's voice did not match her fine facial features.

"Excuse me?"

She lifted her glass, took a sip of her drink, and set the glass back on the cardboard coaster. Bright red lipstick coated the rim of her glass. Her gaze never left him. Her strong rose scented perfume caused his nose to itch. He fought the building sneeze.

"I'm pretty sure they worked for Tony. Don't get me wrong. Tony was a good person, and I really liked him." She paused and sucked in a breath. Her eyes watered. "I warned him that his lifestyle would catch up with him someday. I'm sure he pissed off a lot of husbands and boyfriends through the years." She shook her head and took another sip of her drink.

"What exactly did Tony do for a living, Ms…"

"Barnard. I'm Judy Barnard," she filled in as she extended her hand.

He shook her hand. Her long slim fingers were cold. Her wiry bracelets clinked together, and he couldn't help but notice the large sparkling rings on her fingers. Some stones were clear, some were green. He wondered if the jewels were real.

"So Ms. Barnard, what did Tony do for a living besides bartend?"

She shifted her gaze about the bar before returning it to him. She paused briefly and leaned closer to him. "He ran a male escort service." Even her whisper was raspy.

"Why did he work here then?"

She looked surprised by his question. "This bar is in the professional district. I would imagine he picked up some clients here. You know, when they stopped in for lunch or after work for happy hour."

He kept his gaze on her. Her voice seemed to soften. A hint of sadness passed through her dark eyes. Was she speaking from experience? He wondered how well she knew Tony.

"Were there any others?" Spinelli asked.

Judy frowned. "Others?"

He wondered if there were any more dead cupids they hadn't discovered yet or if there were more at risk on this fine Valentine's Day. "Do you know of any other escorts working for Tony?"

She thought for a moment. "I can't say for sure, but I'd guess there were a few more."

"How do you know?"

She glanced down at her hand and eyed her rings. "Tony likes fine things and somehow seemed to be able to afford them. The more staff you have, the more money you make. Plus, I'd see well- kept, handsome men come in and out of here. Sometimes they'd just come in to talk with Tony for a moment, and they'd leave without getting anything to eat or drink." She paused, looked down, and twisted her bracelets around her wrist. "And sometimes I'd see them pass an envelope between one another."

"What was in the envelope?" Spinelli asked, already knowing the answer.

"Cash, I suppose."

Spinelli nodded in agreement. "Do you know the names of the others who came in to see Tony, or where I can find them?"

She shook her head.

"It's important. Are you sure?"

She nodded. "I'm sure. Sorry."

He believed her. He also believed she mourned Tony's death more than she let on, and he understood.

Sonny made his way back to their end of the bar. "Sorry, it's kind of busy in here tonight."

"No problem," Spinelli cut to the chase, "any chance you know anything about the escort business Tony was running?"

Sonny shot Judy a sideways glance then he looked back at Spinelli. "I'd heard rumors."

"So you don't know for sure?"

Sonny shook his head. "Not my business. I hired him to tend bar, and, as far as I'm concerned, as long as he did that well, we had no problem. If you don't need me for anything else, I'll get back to waiting on my customers."

Spinelli was confident Sonny knew something about Tony's extracurricular activities but probably not much. He seemed like the kind of guy that would just look the other way as long as it didn't affect him, and evidently from Sonny's abrupt end to their conversation, he was done talking about it.

Spinelli, Walker, and Shannon climbed back into the unmarked. Spinelli and Walker debated what to do next. Perhaps if they talked with Mike Carter's sister again she could shed some more light on what he'd been doing with his time lately. At least they could now link the first three cupids together, but there was still no link between them and Joshua Meyers.

Walker signaled and pulled into traffic. Spinelli glanced down at his watch; it was nearly 10:00 p.m. He'd call Cindy Carter first thing in the morning.

Shannon sat silent in the backseat. She'd hardly spoken a word since they'd left the precinct.

This wasn't at all the Valentine's Day Spinelli had planned. He thought about the ring in his pocket. He thought about Shannon kissing Dr. Joshua. His chest hollowed as he recalled the sight of her soft sweet lips touching those of another man. He squeezed his eyes shut hoping to extinguish the unbearable image in his mind. Her lips were meant for him, and only him, as his were for her. He believed her when she said she told Joshua she was seeing someone else, yet his heart still ached at the thought she'd been engaged before. Why did it bother him so much? After all, he had a life before he met her as well.

Spinelli's cell phone buzzed, knocking him out of his trance. He pulled it from its holder on his hip. Marsh's face flashed across the screen. "Spinelli here."

"Yeah, Spinelli, I think I found a connection between Carter and Rosso," Marsh said in a proud tone.

"We got lucky on this end as well. Both Sonny Tomes and one of his regulars have seen Carter and Williams at the bar talking with Rosso at one time or another."

"Oh," Marsh responded with a tinge of disappointment in his tone.

Spinelli figured Marsh was hoping he'd be the hero.

"We're only a couple of minutes out. We'll talk when we get back."

"Okay."

Walker glanced over his shoulder. "You're kind of quiet, Shannon, you doing okay?"

Spinelli turned his head slightly and caught a glimpse of her out of the corner of his eye. She looked pale, sad, and exhausted. He knew he was being a dick and should have been the one to ask her if she was okay, but he just couldn't seem to bring himself to do so. He caught a sideways glance from Walker, confirming his dick status.

Shannon sighed. Her shoulders slumped. "I'm fine. It's all just a bit overwhelming."

"Yeah. Try not to worry. We'll get to the bottom of this," Walker assured, beating Spinelli to it again.

Big fluffy snowflakes fell from the sky as Walker parked the unmarked. The second Spinelli slid out of the car, the crisp, cold, raw wind picked up and slapped him in the face, sending the falling snowflakes sideways and into his eyes. A small set of hands wrapped around his bicep. He didn't need to be able to see to know whose they were. An electrical sensation shot through his arm and then whipped through the rest of his body, instantly warming him in the blustery wind and twenty-degree temperature.

He looked down, catching a glimpse of Shannon's tall red boots, sexy as all get out, but not really made for walking on ice. He slowed his pace to help steady her. He wished he could erase this day and start over. He imagined she wished the same.

Marsh looked up from his table full of laptops when they pushed through the door of the precinct.

"What did you find?" Spinelli asked as he shrugged out of his coat and flung it on the back of his chair.

Marsh pointed at some papers on the table. "Lisa in the IT Department actually found it. After she ran the keystroke program on Chad Williams' computer, she decided to add some sort of filter or query to look for repeat words. Evidently, the word 'angelfish' kept showing up. She traced the word to several email files addressed to 'Angelfish.' Now, the emails are pretty vague, almost as if the people were typing in code or something, but every email seems to reference dates and times. So then I checked Carter's laptop for similar emails, and voila, he had some email correspondence with this 'Angelfish' as well. And in the last email between the two, 'Angelfish' told Carter to dress as cupid for his meeting." Marsh sighed. "Oddly, Rosso's laptop shows no emails to or from 'Angelfish,' but maybe he has another computer or device we didn't find."

Marsh paused and looked at Spinelli as if he should know exactly about what he was talking.

"How exactly then are you tying Rosso into these emails?" Spinelli asked.

Marsh rolled his eyes. "For crissake. Don't you get it? He's 'Angelfish.' It's so evident."

"Enlighten us."

"Remember the fish from Rosso's apartment?"

"Yeah."

"Those were Resplendent Angelfish," Marsh stated with confidence.

"Okay?"

Marsh sucked in a breath of annoyance. "Resplendent Angelfish are hardy fish that adapt well to aquarium life; however, they're semi-aggressive and tend to form groups comprised of one male and several females. Who else would be 'Angelfish' other than Rosso?"

Walker nodded. "It all seems to make sense, between this and what we found out at Sonny's."

Spinelli filled Marsh in on the conversation they had with Sonny and Judy. "But we still have a few missing links. How does Meyers tie in? Who contracted with Rosso's service to kill four cupids? Furthermore, only cupids Shannon once dated." Spinelli's gaze shifted to the wings, bow, and quiver full of arrows on his desk. "And who in the hell had enough control of the situation to get me to dress as cupid as well?"

"Don't forget about Lady Lily." Marsh added.

"Who?" Spinelli questioned.

"Lady Lily. The person Williams emailed and agreed to meet with at the Morgan Bank building this morning."

Walker nodded. "Oh yes, the flower of death person." His comment evidently conceded that his earlier recollection of the orchid being the flower of death was incorrect.

"Actually, as it turns out, not only are lilies the flowers of death, but they are also known well for their use in aquariums," Marsh added.

"And how is that pertinent?" Spinelli cut in, wanting to kick himself the second the question came out of his mouth because he knew, rather than just cutting to the chase, Marsh would probably embark on some sort of long drawn-out useless explanation as usual.

"Well, you see, the lily's broad leaves produce shaded areas in the aquarium which encourage shy or reclusive fish species to actively forage in open view. But the problem with planting lilies in aquariums is that if they are left unattended, their leaves will grow large and block all the light from the understory and kill those plants. One of the most common lilies offered for aquarium use is the dwarf lily. Go figure. Dwarf."

They all just stared at Marsh.

The silence encouraged him to continue. "You know, dwarf lily and dwarf angelfish. And think about it. She sucks the men out into the open, then wham, kills off everything in her path."

"But who is Lady Lily?" Spinelli asked, unable to hide the frustration from his tone.

Marsh leaned back and crossed his arms over his chest. "I didn't get that far yet. I'm just…just showing the connection."

Spinelli inhaled deeply and slowly then emptied his lungs. "Okay, thank you for that, Marsh, there's two minutes of my life I can't have back." Spinelli shifted his gaze to Shannon. "When was the last time Meyers was in the states?"

"I can't say for sure. All I know is that it's been a couple of years since I've seen him. He'd send a postcard periodically, but even those came less often as time went by."

Walker flipped open a file folder and studied its contents. "Hmm."

Spinelli craned his neck to look in the folder as well. "Did you find something?"

"No, not really. I was just looking at the vics' ages trying to link them somehow. But it's not working. Rosso was 35, Williams was 36, Carter was 28, and Meyers was just shy of 33." Walker looked up from the file and glanced at Shannon. "So Meyers was in his last year of medical school when you dated him?"

She nodded.

"What school did he go to?"

Shannon cocked her head to the side. "The University of Madison."

Walker shifted his gaze to Spinelli. "Didn't Bethany go to Madison?"

"I'm not sure."

Walker squinted and stared at the crime board. He ran his hand over his five o'clock shadow and then held his chin. "You know, I think it says Madison on the diploma hanging behind her desk." His gaze shifted back to Spinelli. "How old is Bethany?"

Spinelli shrugged. "Somewhere around my age. 32 or so."

"She's the right age. Maybe she knew Meyers. Maybe she kept in touch, or maybe she knows who he may have kept in touch with," Walker commented as he stepped closer to the crime board. "You know, it's just too coincidental that Meyers returned home on the day of all these murders and then gets murdered himself."

"And murdered wearing a cupid outfit," Marsh added. "Could he have been double crossed?"

"What do you mean?" Spinelli asked.

"I mean, was he partially responsible for the murders of Carter, Rosso, and Williams, and then got murdered himself because the plan went bad or the orchestrator of the plan wanted to tie up loose ends?"

"It's as good a theory as any right now."

Spinelli pulled his cell phone from his hip and tapped the screen.

"Who are you calling?" Marsh asked.

"Bethany."

Marsh glanced at his watch. "It's after 10:00, you know. We could just pick this back up in the morning."

"Do you have someplace important to be?"

Marsh shook his head and shifted his eyes to Walker. "No, I don't, but maybe other people do."

"You got that right," Captain Jackson blurted as she walked up to the crime board. "I'd rather be at home, but I've got the Mayor breathing down my neck over this cupid case. Evidently, the media is having a field day over the murders and our lack of response." She shifted her annoyed gaze to Spinelli, pinning him in place. A shiver ran up his spine. Her small frame never kept her from showing who was in charge and demanding the utmost respect. She perched her hands on her narrow hips. Her nostrils flared with each breath she took. "So what do we have here, Spinelli?"

Spinelli glanced at his phone screen. His call to Bethany went to voicemail. He looked up to find all eyes on him. "She's not answering."

"And you're surprised by that why?" Marsh asked as he chuckled. "The woman despises you," he assured Spinelli as if hadn't already had a clue.

The impatient tapping of Jackson's foot drew Spinelli's attention. "What?"

"I asked you a question? Where are you guys at with the cupid case?"

Spinelli's gaze shifted to the crime board, then back to Jackson. He sighed heavily. "We don't have anything other than the fact they were all poisoned by cyanide ingestion. We've just now linked the first three cupids together, but not the fourth." He glanced back at his phone. "And just now I was trying to contact Bethany. She may be able to shed some light on Meyers, the fourth Cupid, and perhaps help us link him to the other three, but she didn't answer her phone."

"Our Bethany? The pathologist?" Jackson asked as her head snapped in Marsh's direction. She shot him a scowl. "Is that who you were talking about when I walked up?"

Marsh nodded.

"Well that doesn't make any sense at all," Jackson added as she turned her attention back to Spinelli.

"Why does that surprise you? I thought every Tom, Dick, and Harry knew how she felt about me," Spinelli stated as he avoided making any sort of eye contact with Shannon at this point. He wondered why he felt guilty as they talked about his old girlfriend, especially since he'd caught Shannon kissing one of her old flames earlier.

Jackson pointed at the heart shaped box of chocolates on his desk. "She dropped that off for you a couple of hours ago. Right before I left to go home. She seemed all cheery at that time."

All eyes shifted to the box of chocolates.

Spinelli stepped over to his desk and lifted the lid. They looked like normal chocolates. Everyone else hovered around the desk and leaned in.

"Bethany?" he whispered.

"I'll get them to the lab," Walker said as he gloved his hand and gingerly took the lid from Spinelli.

Jackson cleared her throat. "Okay, but it will take several days at best to get the results."

She flashed Spinelli a sympathetic look. He shifted his gaze to his feet. God how he hated the sympathetic look. He'd received it too many times as a child. Every time he entered a new foster home, the foster parents flashed him the same look he'd just received from Jackson. If he never saw that sympathetic look again, it would be too soon. Was he that pathetic?

"I'll send a black and white to Bethany's house. We'll bring her in for questioning," Jackson added.

"I'll have IT check her emails. See if we can find anything there," Marsh said, his voice somber. It was one of the few times Spinelli didn't detect cockiness or sarcasm in Marsh's voice.

Spinelli stared down at his desk where the box of chocolates once sat. Could Bethany really have orchestrated this whole thing? Could she have killed four people? And did she really want him dead as well? His core chilled at the thought. They'd only gone out a few times, never even slept together. His vision blurred as sweat ran down his back.

He tried to live a good life. He tried to be a good person, yet he may have been the reason for the deaths of Tony Rosso, Mike Carter, Chad Williams, and Joshua Meyers. And poor Shannon. What had he done to her?

Maybe he was no better than his drug addicted mother after all. Was he ultimately responsible for her death as well? Was he simply too much for her to handle. Perhaps if she hadn't had him at such a young age, she wouldn't have had to sell herself on street corners to support herself, him, and her awful drug fetish. There were times he hated her for what she'd done to him as a child, leaving him home alone to fend for himself for days at a time for as far back as he could remember. Drugs seemed to be more important to her than he was. He recalled the countless foster homes he'd spent time in when she wasn't up for the task of raising him. Some weren't so bad, but others were awful. He closed his eyes at the last memory of her. He was sixteen, and he'd come home to their run-down, filthy apartment to find her lying dead on the couch. Drug overdose. His chest constricted. His heart fought to beat.

Spinelli flinched at the sensation of warmth that crept up his arm as Shannon wrapped her small hand around his bicep. He couldn't look at her. He couldn't risk it. Tears stung his eyes, but he refused to let them fall. He hadn't cried since he was six years old, and he wasn't about to start now. Shame penetrated every cell in his body.

"I know what you're thinking, and this isn't your fault," she said as she lightly squeezed his arm.

He still couldn't look at her.

She tugged his arm. "Nick, look at me."

His gaze drifted to her. Her warm eyes looked up at him. He loved her beautiful green eyes. He'd never grow tired of staring into them. She reached up and placed her small hands on his cheeks. His already burning cheeks warmed even more.

Her beautiful full lips parted. "This is not your fault. You didn't do this," she stated firmly as if in full belief of her words. Her gaze didn't waiver. God, how he loved her. Too bad he needed to let her go. He seemed to always hurt those around him, and he couldn't bear the thought of hurting her any more than he already had today.

He stepped back, pulling himself from her hold. The hurt in her expression nearly killed him. But it had to be done. She would be better off without him. Her hand dropped to her side.

"Don't do that, Nick," she whispered, her eyes pleaded.

He felt like such a bastard.

Chapter Thirteen

Spinelli urged Shannon to let the patrol officer take her home. She wouldn't budge. *Stubborn redhead!*

The sound of women's heels clicking against the hardwood floor drew Spinelli's attention. Captain Jackson stepped up to him and Shannon. "The officers with Bethany just pulled up. I want you two to make yourselves scarce while they bring her in. And Spinelli, I know I don't need to say this, but you can watch from the other room."

He opened his mouth to protest he'd like nothing more than to interrogate the shit out of the woman who likely orchestrated this whole thing, but then thought better of it. He knew Jackson was right. He'd likely not be able to maintain his cool and get the job done, and it was likely that Bethany would be more responsive and cooperative with someone else.

"Who's going to do it? Walker?"

"No, I think I'll take the first go around on this one."

Jackson didn't say it, but Spinelli figured she thought maybe Bethany would respond better to a woman.

Shannon rested her hand on Spinelli's shoulder. "I'll wait for you in the lunchroom.

A nod was all he could muster before he headed in the direction of the small dimly lit room adjacent to the interrogation room. He stood in front of the two-way mirror staring into the next room as he waited for the suspect to arrive. Walker entered a moment later.

"Where's Marsh?" Spinelli asked.

"He's with Lisa in IT. They're still combing through Bethany's emails, looking for anything that ties her to the victims."

Spinelli shifted his gaze back to the empty interrogation room. The room was dimly lit and clean. A metal table sat in the center. It's color a gloomy gray. The room was so tiny one was hardly able to walk around the table. One burnt orange, plastic chair sat on each of the long sides of the rectangular table, making the room even tighter. He hated those old, ugly, uncomfortable chairs. He was sure they'd been in that room since the beginning of time. But those crappy old chairs did exactly what they were supposed to which was to keep the suspect from becoming too comfortable. He hated the smell of the room, too. The odor reminded him of a musty basement.

He wished they would just get here so they could get this over with. He glanced at Walker who'd partially propped himself up on the table behind him. His arms were crossed over his chest, and he stared through the two-way mirror into the empty interrogation room. The door to the interrogation room opened, drawing Spinelli's attention.

Bethany stepped into the room then looked back at Captain Jackson who followed on her heels. Jackson gestured toward one of the chairs, and Bethany slid it out from under the table and took a seat. She scooted the chair up to the table and rested her arms on the tabletop. She drummed her fingers as if annoyed.

Jackson remained standing on the same side of the table in which Bethany sat; about an arm's length away. Spinelli was sure Jackson stood between Bethany and the door by design. It was an interrogation strategy. The suspect would have to go through the interrogator if she tried to make a run for it.

"Bethany, did the officers tell you why we wanted you to come down to the station?" Jackson asked. Her voice was soft and controlled.

Bethany nodded. "They mentioned something about me knowing one of the dead cupids."

"That's right. How did you know him?"

"What do you mean? How did I know him? He worked in this building. Mostly I saw him in the parking lot when we arrived in the morning or left at night."

"You're talking about Chad Williams?" Jackson questioned.

"Yeah."

Spinelli arched a brow and looked at Walker. "Question diversion?" An attempt often made by suspects to get the interrogator to move in a different direction.

"Could be."

Jackson's gaze stayed on Bethany. "Oh, so then you know two of the cupids."

"What?"

"Joshua Meyers. You knew him as well?"

"No."

Jackson arched a brow. "Hmm, he didn't look at all familiar to you when you examined him?"

"No."

"That's odd. You'd think after all those years in medical school together you would have run into him at one time or another."

"Well, it's not like we were the only two in the graduating class."

"You're right," Jackson said as she cocked her head to the side. "What do you know about tropical fish?"

Bethany studied Jackson for a few beats. She looked puzzled. "They're pretty."

"That's it? Nothing else?"

Bethany's jaw clenched. "The males tend to be prettier than the females."

"Does that upset you?"

Bethany huffed, leaned back in her chair, and crossed her arms over her chest. "Why would it? Why would I care?"

"I don't know. You just seem bothered by that."

"Whatever," Bethany replied with a roll of her eyes and the attitude of a teenager who'd just been set straight by her parents. "You brought me down here to talk about fish?" she questioned, her tone still juvenile.

Spinelli's eyes narrowed. *She's getting a little testy already. That was quick.* Jackson's twenty plus years on the force really showed during times like these. Her small frame never precluded her from getting the job done. And her eyes. Spinelli was sure he'd confess to anything if her small dark eyes zoned in on him the way they zoned in on the suspects. She was a strong woman. He always admired her for that. His old partner, Mad Dog, had told him early on to make sure to stay on her good side. Good bosses like her were hard to come by. And though she expected a lot from her staff, she stood behind them one hundred percent when the shit hit the fan.

A knock sounded on the interrogation room door. Both Jackson and Bethany's heads turned in that direction. Marsh poked his head in and motioned for Jackson. She stepped into the doorway and Marsh whispered something to her.

She looked back at Bethany. "I'll be right back."

Bethany shrugged.

Jackson and Marsh entered the room in which Spinelli and Walker resided. Marsh looked like he was ready to explode. *What did he find?*

Marsh flopped a stack of papers on the table. He fanned the stack. Yellow highlights appeared sporadically throughout the documents.

"What are those?" Jackson asked as she placed her finger on one of the highlighted areas.

"These are printouts of Bethany's Internet records. Evidently she has a hotmail email account she logs into on occasion for personal business during work hours. She was smart enough not to use her work email account, but evidently she's not smart enough to know that IT has records of all computer activity generated by all work computers," he shook his head, "and she's got a doctorate."

"What are you trying to tell us?" Jackson asked, cutting to the chase.

"I had IT run their keystroke search program on Bethany's computer to see if she had any correspondence with 'Angelfish' like Williams had. All the highlighted areas are just that, emails to or from someone called 'Angelfish.' And just like we found on Williams' and Carter's computers, the conversations seem vague, but do reference a particular date and some specific early morning hours, the date being February 14th."

All sound faded from Spinelli's ears with the exception of his thudding heart and his hissing lungs. He fought to refill his lungs; it seemed to be a struggle. He knew going in to Bethany's questioning there was a good chance she was involved in this whole mess. He'd hoped for some sort of miracle that he was wrong. But Marsh had likely just added the final nail to the coffin, and ultimately, he knew he was responsible for the deaths of Rosso, Carter, Williams, and Meyers.

His dates with Bethany replayed through his mind. They were just dates, nothing special. No flowers, no expensive dinners, no weekends away, and no sex. He thought about things he had said to her. He couldn't come up with one conversation where he'd led her to believe there was more to their relationship than he thought.

The voices of Jackson, Marsh, and Walker eased back into his eardrums, slowly growing louder with each passing moment. Marsh was mumbling something about a Beta fish being temperamental and aggressive. He went on to explain that the females are normally shorter, have thicker bellies, less finnage, and are less vibrant in color than the males. What the hell was he talking about? He was a walking encyclopedia of useless information.

"They're also known as a Siamese Fighting Fish. They flare out their gill plates towards other fish to show hostility or when they feel threatened," Marsh added.

"What does that have to do with anything?" Spinelli asked unable to camouflage his impatience.

"Weren't you listening? That's what I just explained. In her emails to 'Angelfish' she uses the call name of 'Betta' fish. I'm just saying that she probably picked that name for a reason. It has a similar behavior pattern to her. Just like Rosso choosing 'Angelfish' has a similar behavior pattern to him."

"Oh."

"That's all good and well, we've got her, but none of this ties her to Meyers."

Marsh beamed. He was on a roll. "Those don't," he flipped to the last page in the small stack of papers and tapped his finger on the final yellow highlighted section, "but this one does."

Simultaneously everyone leaned forward to get a better look. Among the hundreds of characters on the page the word "Eros" appeared highlighted in yellow.

"Eros?" Spinelli questioned

"I had Lisa in IT run their search program on the word 'cupid' as well 'Angelfish' but nothing came up. Then for kicks and giggles, I had Lisa run the program on 'Eros' and voila, here you have it. She typed an email, yesterday, to someone going by the name of Eros."

Everyone continued to stare at Marsh.

"For crissake, don't you guys know anything about Roman or Greek mythology?"

Jackson's toe tapping evidently urged Marsh to enlighten them further. That was her thing; tapping her toe, and it always seemed to work.

Marsh rolled his eyes. "In Roman mythology, Cupid is the god of desire. His Greek counterpart is Eros," he paused briefly, "and just a little FYI, in case it ever comes up again, Cupid is known in Latin as Amor."

"Wait a minute. This morning when I asked you about cupid you didn't know shit."

Marsh chuckled. "I Googled it this afternoon."

He's such a smartass.

Jackson looked up at Marsh. "Is there anything else of use in the email?"

Marsh's smile stretched. "Just that she was going to pick up Eros from the airport at 11:00 a.m. today."

"Christ, she's making this too easy. It's almost as if she wanted to get caught," Jackson commented, "but how or why did she bring him in from Nicaragua. She already pulled together three of Shannon's exes. Why did he agree to come?"

"I'm guessing she wanted a full-sweep. Shannon invaded her territory, and Meyers was the only one left. The rest of them were at her fingertips." Walker commented as he ran his hand over his face.

Spinelli could nearly see the wheels turning in Walker's head.

Walker pressed on. "She put a lot of planning into this it must have taken weeks if not months. She staged all the murders to take place before Shannon would arrive at work, probably hoping she would have no alibi. But due to Meyers' flight time, she couldn't get that one done before 8:00 a.m." Walker cocked a brow, "How do you suppose she got him to agree come here to see Shannon?"

"Perhaps he's the jealous type," Marsh interjected as he glanced at Spinelli. Shannon told us how he didn't seem to take her breakup seriously. "Maybe Bethany got word to him of the seriousness of her relationship with Spinelli, and he came home to interfere. Up until

Spinelli entered the picture, she hadn't had any serious prospects; therefore, Meyers didn't have to worry about losing her while he was away. He probably figured she was just sitting here patiently awaiting his return."

Walker stepped toward the two-way mirror. Spinelli shifted his gaze to the mirror as well. Bethany chewed on her nails. Had Jackson's extended absence from the room made her nervous?

"I suppose that theory is possible. Let's see if I can get anything else out of her," Jackson said as she grabbed the stack of papers off the table, stuffed them into a manila folder, and exited the room.

Spinelli, Walker, and Marsh stood with their noses pressed against the two-way mirror. Jackson entered the interrogation room with the folder tucked under her arm.

Bethany's brown-eyed gaze shifted to Jackson. She stopped chewing on her fingernails and rested her arms on the table.

"Let's see. Where were we? Oh yes, you were telling me you didn't know much about tropical fish and that you didn't know Dr. Joshua Meyers. Is that correct?"

Bethany sighed. "Yes, I think we've already established that." She cocked her jaw and ran her hand through her short, brown, wispy hair. She seemed more annoyed than nervous by the questioning.

"Pathological liar?" Spinelli questioned as he looked at Walker and Marsh.

"Could be," Marsh replied.

Jackson pulled the folder from under her arm and flipped it open. She stared at the contents for a while. Silence—an interrogation ploy.

Bethany picked at her fingernails then resumed chewing on them.

"Maybe she's a neurotic?" Spinelli questioned.

"That would seem to fit. Difficulty with relationships, functions in society as a fairly normal person, and she always appears somewhat nervous and tense," Marsh recapped.

"And extremely hyperactive," Spinelli added. "Part of what turned me off. That and the fact she always seemed so unhappy."

Spinelli turned his attention back to the activity in the interrogation room.

Jackson shifted her gaze from the folder back to Bethany. "Do you have a hotmail account?"

"Doesn't everyone?"

"The question is do you have one?"

"Yes."

"What name do you go by when you use that account?"

Bethany rolled her eyes. "I use my name, bdier at hotmail.com."

"Hmm, do you use any other hotmail accounts?"

"Nope."

"Does anyone else have access to your office computer?"

Bethany's eyes widened. Her fists balled, and she dropped them to her lap. Spinelli assumed it was a deliberate maneuver to hide her anxiety.

"Bethany, does anyone else have access to your office computer?" Jackson repeated.

"I don't think so," her voice squeaked in reply.

Jackson pulled a paper from the folder and set it on the table in front of Bethany. "So then likely it was you who drafted the email to Eros, using the name of Betta?" Jackson questioned as she pointed to the paper and returned her gaze to meet Bethany's.

Bethany's eyes never wavered from Jackson. Not once during the brief silence that followed Jackson's question did Bethany look down at the papers. Spinelli suspected she had no need to.

"I think I'll call my attorney now," Bethany replied through gritted teeth.

Jackson closed the file and scooped it up. "Okay. I'll send an officer in. He'll take you to holding, and you can make your call."

* * * *

Betta tilted her head back and stared at the ceiling while she waited for the officer to come get her. The corners of her mouth tugged upward. She'd succeeded. Two months of tedious planning, and it finally all came to fruition. The plan was foolproof. Any moron could have carried it out. But she did it. She did it herself and couldn't have been more pleased with the outcome. She inhaled slowly and deeply and let her breath out. She felt cleansed. She'd rid the world of four problems.

She'd set out to make this one hell of a Valentine's Day for the ever famous womanizing Nick Spinelli and his whore girlfriend, Shannon

O'Hara. Even though she knew she'd never win the heart of Nick Spinelli, the woman he loved would surely be through with him now as well. There was no way Shannon O'Hara would stay with a man that caused her so much grief. From now until the end of time, every time Spinelli and O'Hara looked at each other, they'd be reminded of their special Valentine's Day.

Laughter rang from Betta's mouth. She would have given anything to see the look on Spinelli's face a moment ago when realization set in that he was the cause of death of all of Shannon's past lovers. She'd considered poisoning him as well, but in the end, she figured the guilt associated with the blood on his hands was a more appropriate punishment for him. He'd need to learn to live with this for the rest of his life. The thought warmed her like a down quilt.

Betta rolled her eyes. Poor, sweet, innocent Shannon. She was just as much to blame for this entire mess, all pure and nice all the time. Nobody's that nice. Betta's eye twitched. She pressed her fingers to it. It wouldn't stop. Thoughts of Shannon always made her eye twitch. She'd thought the day's events would have taken care of the involuntary annoying movement. She shrugged. *Oh well.* She'd worry about that later.

Betta lifted her head from the back of the chair, leaned forward, and fixed her eyes on the two-way mirror. She wondered if Spinelli stared at her through the glass. She wondered if he was angry with her or sad. It didn't matter. She'd made her point and made it quite clearly.

Her reflection in the glass faded, and Mike Carter's light brown eyes suddenly stared back at her. Mike had sad, desperate eyes. They looked nothing now as they'd looked in the Prom picture Betta found on the Internet. He and Shannon stood up on their pedestal looking all smug, like they were some sort of special couple, just because they'd made the court. Facebook made it so easy to find Shannon's high school sweetheart. Betta shook her head. When will people learn not to post so much personal information for the world to see? *Idiots.*

Mike's new image was enough to make Betta feel sorry for him. Poor guy, lost his job and had to resort to selling himself for bread and butter. Betta smiled. Adrenaline shot through her veins. Mike was definitely worth the $2,000 she'd paid him. He had slow hands and quickly figured out how to push her buttons, not just once, but twice. She'd actually considered sparing him, figuring it was a shame to remove him from the grasp of women. But hell, he was just a male slut selling himself.

She'd offered to drive him home when they'd finished. He'd accepted the ride. She'd fed him the chocolates she'd hand-prepared for him as she drove. It didn't take long for the desperation and sadness to drain from of his eyes.

Betta leaned back in her chair and crossed her arms over her chest. The more she thought about it, she realized she'd probably done Mike a huge favor, releasing him from his pathetic, useless life. But she did feel kind of bad, leaving him the way she did, propped up on a snow bank wearing nothing but wings for the whole world to see. She shrugged. *Oh well.* She knew she had to get rid of him quickly, so she'd pushed him out of the car in the first available alley. Tony was probably already waiting for her. She'd scheduled her appointments pretty tight. She had a lot to accomplish in a twenty-four hour period.

Betta propped her elbow up on the table and rested her chin on her palm as she continued to stare forward. Mike's image faded, and Tony Rosso's handsome chiseled features now shined in front of her. His perfect white smile nearly lit up the interrogation room.

Self-esteem had not been an issue for Rosso. He oozed confidence in everything he did. If only Rosso really knew. Yeah, he brought her to orgasm, but he was so mechanical. She'd felt as though he were following an operator's manual as they humped on his boss' desk. She'd expected more from a professional who'd been in the business for a while. But she had to admit, the guy was good-looking and built to perfection, and what he did for that set of wings was a crime in itself. Her fingertips burned at the recollection of how his hot skin and hard-muscled body felt as she ran her hands over him. And his scent. She wasn't sure she'd ever smelled anything as tantalizing in her life. Between his captivating scent and the sight of his wings fluttering in unison as he pumped inside her, she'd nearly forgotten why she was there. His over-confidence annoyed her and reminded her of her purpose.

When the time had come for her to take control and get the job done, they'd switched positions. She took pleasure in feeding him her handmade chocolates as she rode him like the man whore he was. Had he no shame, pimping out desperate souls like he did?

Betta remembered glancing at the clock. She needed to hurry. Chad Williams was waiting for her. She fed Tony another chocolate. He coughed and then choked. She climbed off him and watched as his olive colored cheeks turned red as a fire truck. He'd sat up, as if that would help. But the coughing continued and was soon followed by vomiting. It didn't take long for his body to fall back onto the desk and convulse. His body stilled. His once smug eyes stared emptily at the ceiling.

Betta hoped her Aunt Judy wouldn't be upset with her if and when she found out that Betta had killed Rosso. Judy spoke highly of her paid lover. Hell, the way Betta saw it, Judy was just as much to blame for Rosso's death. If she and Betta hadn't shared a bottle of champagne at Shannon's Uncle Bernie's bar the night of Judy's 60th birthday, Betta would have never happened upon Shannon's short involvement with Rosso. The information meant nothing to Betta at the time, over one and one-half years ago, but she remembered it when needed. She recalled how jealous her aunt acted that night as they watched Rosso behind the bar. Judy worried that someday a fine young woman would truly peak Tony's interest, and cause him to leave the business.

Betta talked to her aunt shortly before the police knocked on her door so she knew Spinelli, Walker, and Marsh had questioned her aunt about Rosso at Sonny's Bar. At that time, her aunt didn't have a clue she was the one who killed Rosso. Judy was sure to find out. *Oh well, it needed to be done.*

Rosso's image in the two-way mirror transitioned to that of Chad Williams. Chad had surprised her. She still wondered why he joined Rosso's team of male hookers. It wasn't like he was broke. He had a good job with decent pay and benefits. He seemed like a nice, regular, clock-punching Joe. She'd heard rumors he had a gambling problem, so maybe that's why he did it. Perhaps he had needed to get a bookie off his back. In the end it really didn't matter why he'd done it, it worked out well for her.

Chad simply did as he she'd asked. His touch was soft and sweet. He seemed like the marrying kind. In fact, she wondered why a guy like him wasn't married already. She'd never really talked with him at work.

She'd see him come in and out of the building in the morning when she arrived at work or in the afternoon when she left. He always carried a clipboard in his hand. The same metal clipboard she saw laying on top the bags of plaster powder next to where they screwed. Perhaps she'd take the clipboard when she left, a little remembrance of him. Why not take it. He wouldn't need it any longer. Nah, she didn't need the clipboard. She had a better remembrance piece already; a group photo of all the attendees from the summer picnic, the summer before last. Though he was city employee, he came as Shannon's guest to the county picnic. In the photo he stood next to Shannon with his arm draped over her shoulder. *How sweet.*

When he stood to dress, she'd decided it was time. He couldn't be found with his clothes on. That just wouldn't be right. Before he had a chance to dress, she retrieved the small heart shaped box of chocolates from her handbag, opened it, pulled the only rectangle one from the box, and popped it into her mouth. She held the box out to him. Without hesitation he took one, one of her special round, handmade chocolates that filled the remaining slots in the box. He'd popped the chocolate into his mouth and chewed only a couple of times before he swallowed it, not taking nearly enough time to savor the smooth chocolate. Betta wondered why they didn't ever take the time to enjoy the little things. It would behoove them.

She'd offered him another chocolate. He had nearly inhaled that one as well. When he bent over to pick up his pants he'd started to cough and then choke. She'd stood by as he vomited several times before he fell to the floor. His body shook. His soft brown eyes darkened as they nearly bulged out of his head. He stilled. It was time to go.

Betta squeezed her eyes shut and opened them to find Dr. Joshua Meyers' mug staring back at her from the two-way mirror. Joshua was built differently than the others. The first three cupids resembled Spinelli. They were tall and muscular. They had dark complexions and brown eyes. Joshua was wiry, had a light complexion, and bright blue eyes. And he simply wasn't as handsome as the others were. Betta wondered what Shannon had seen in him, other than him being a doctor.

Fortunately for Betta, Joshua was the jealous type and was easily manipulated. She'd remembered that from college. He'd dated her roommate and slept with every girl he could get his hands on, yet her roommate wasn't allowed to date anyone else. Betta never understood why her roommate was so upset when he dumped her for Shannon. He never treated her right.

Though Meyers was a womanizer through and through, he'd nearly hopped the next plane when she'd told him about Shannon's serious relationship with Spinelli. Betta could tell from their phone conversation that he wasn't fully committed to Shannon, but he didn't want anyone else to have her, either. He had planned to come back home to her at some point when he was ready, and he fully expected her to be there waiting for him.

Who in the hell did Meyers think he was? Betta huffed. In her book, he wasn't good looking enough to be this way, but he did have charisma. She wondered why a guy like him would volunteer for a church mission trip. It didn't make any sense. Was it guilt? Was he trying to buy his way into heaven after all the cheating he'd done? Betta shook her head. She knew the truth. He was either trying to bag some foreign women before he came back home to settle down with Shannon, or perhaps he was simply just taking advantage of the opportunity laid before him; living in a mission community comprised of mostly young female volunteers. People get lonely, and have needs, even the pure and innocent ones. Betta was sure Meyers basked in the collection pool of innocent and pure women at his fingertips in the mission community. The fact that Meyers dated people like Shannon and Betta's college roommate, supported Betta's theory; Meyers liked corrupting the innocents. It was a little game he liked to play. *Asshole!*

Betta thought about screwing Meyers before she did him in, but the thrill of the hunt was too strong. She'd simply wanted him dead. Because he was such a dick, she did suppress her urgency and took the time to coax him into his wings first. She wanted to tease him, and lead him on a bit, before she gave him the opportunity to find out if his voluntary mission work bought him passage through the pearly gates.

Betta pulled the wings from the bag she'd brought with her to Meyer's hotel room. She'd saved him the trouble of having to pick up his own cupid costume for the fundraiser. He had no time for such things. His time, since he arrived so late on this special day, was better spent manipulating Shannon and helping to make her look guilty as sin in terms of murdering her past lovers.

Betta smiled. She was having so much fun. She handed the wings to Meyers before she reached her hands behind her back and pulled down the zipper of her dress. Her dress fell to the floor exposing her bare breasts and the small patch of material covering her fresh Brazilian Shave. She shimmied out of her thong and by the time she looked up again Meyers wore nothing but wings. He was such a player; so easy, and such an idiot for a man with a doctorate.

Meyers opened his mouth to receive the piece of chocolate Betta held. He'd eaten his candy like a good boy, then sat on the bed and patted the spot next to him before he hurled, fell back, jerked, and stilled. His once piercing blue eyes turned as dark as Lake Michigan in winter.

Betta's icy veins warmed at the sight of him sprawled out on the bed. He'd been such an easy target—almost too easy.

Betta leaned back in her chair and stared into space as she basked in her pleasurable thoughts of her good day. She nearly patted herself on the back for a job well done. She'd gotten a lot done in a short period of time. She'd saved the female gender from a great deal of potential heartache today by taking out four womanizing man whores. The corners of her mouth twitched upward. She couldn't suppress her smile even if she tried. Sheer excitement rushed through her veins at the speed of light. She had one last trick up her sleeve to pull off before the clock struck midnight, and she was in the perfect position to get it done.

* * * *

A uniformed officer entered the interrogation room and cuffed Bethany, but not before she blew a kiss in the direction of the two-way mirror, winked, and mouthed, "All for you, Spinelli."

Her words were unmistakable.

Hysterical laughter rang from her lips as the officer guided her out of the room and took her to holding. The shrill pitch echoing in the precinct was deafening.

Marsh caught Spinelli's gaze and shook his head. "She's one hell of a crazy bitch."

All eyes drifted to the Captain as she entered the room. Marsh informed her of Bethany's last actions in the interrogation room. Jackson nodded. She didn't seem surprised.

A few beats of silence passed. He was sure the others were of like mind. Just when they'd thought they'd seen everything something like this happens.

Jackson broke the uncomfortable silence. "Well, I guess our work is done here." Her gaze shifted to Spinelli. "I'm sorry, Nick."

"Me, too."

She glanced at her watch. "I can't believe the time already. So much for our Valentine's Day. I'll see you all in the morning."

Jackson hadn't taken two steps away from them before they heard the 911 page come through from holding. They were calling for medical assistance.

Spinelli ran in that direction. It didn't take a rocket scientist to know who the call was for. Walker, Marsh, and Jackson were on his heels.

The young night-shift officer guarding holding buzzed them through in stride. They stopped in front of Bethany's cell. She lay convulsing on the floor in her own vomit. Her eyes looked like they were about to pop out of her head. The acidic stench of her vomit scorched Spinelli's lungs.

Within seconds, the EMTs pushed their way through. The officer attempting to help Bethany rose to her feet and stepped out of their way.

"What happened?" the older of the EMTs asked the officer.

"I don't know…I locked her in the cell and started walking away. I hadn't taken but a few steps before she began to cough. I looked back at her to find her face already as red as a fire truck. Then she vomited several times, fell to the floor, and started convulsing. At that point I called for you guys."

The EMT looked at Spinelli. He stood the closest to them. Jackson, Walker, and Marsh had been smart enough to keep more distance between themselves and the cell. Spinelli swiped his sweaty palms over his thighs. Sweat beaded on his temples and upper lip. His mind was telling him what to say, but it was if the words wouldn't come out of his mouth. The EMT's look intensified, snapping him back into reality.

"Cyanide. She may have poisoned herself."

Bethany's body suddenly stilled. The EMTs strapped oxygen to her and loaded her onto the stretcher. Within seconds they were gone.

With the exception of Shannon, who still waited in the lunchroom for Spinelli, they all gathered in Jackson's tiny office awaiting the news on Bethany. Minutes later Jackson's desk phone rang. All eyes shifted to her.

"Captain Jackson...uh huh...I see...okay."

Her sympathetic brown-eyed gaze landed on Spinelli. She didn't need to speak for him to know the outcome, but she did anyhow.

"Bethany died en route."

Though that had likely been Bethany's plan all along, it didn't make Spinelli feel any better.

Chapter Fourteen

Shannon sat quietly in the passenger seat of Spinelli's truck, staring out the windshield. She hadn't said a word since he told her about the interview with Bethany and her untimely death. He was sure Shannon blamed him for this disastrous day.

Outside of waking up with her in his bed, not one thing went as planned. He thought about the ring in his pocket. There was no way he could attempt to go there now, maybe not ever. A sharp pain sliced through his heart at the thought, but he was simply bad news for her. She'd probably never forgive him anyway no less accept a proposal from him. She deserved better.

He parked his truck, sprang out, and hustled around to the passenger side to get the door for her. When he opened the door, she didn't move. It's like she was in a trance.

"Shannon, sweetheart, you're home."

She flinched. "What?" she asked as she turned her head in his direction. Her eyes still watered.

Spinelli extended his hand toward her. "We're here, come on. Let's get you inside."

Without hesitation she slipped her hand into his. That had to be a good sign. What was he thinking? It would be so much easier to walk away from her if she blamed him and pushed him away. Then he wouldn't have to be strong about it. He could just take his beating, tuck his tail between his legs, and go home to wallow in self-pity.

He ran his fingers over the numeric keypad next to the glass door of her apartment building. She'd given him the code weeks ago. The buzzer sounded, and he pushed the door open for her to pass through. He recalled the first time he held that door for her, a mere couple of months ago. She'd tried to brush him off in that very spot, but he ignored her attempt and proceeded to walk her all the way to her apartment door. Before he was able to leave, she invited him in for some of the gingerbread cookies she'd baked the night before. Well, maybe she didn't exactly invite him in willingly. Her cute, little, old neighbors may have played matchmaker that night. But nonetheless, he was invited in for cookies. He knew, without doubt, that very night, his life would never be the same.

He stifled a chuckle. Though now was not the time for laughing, he couldn't help himself as he recalled the craziness he'd undergone over the past two months since he'd met her. He'd gone undercover as Santa Claus to protect her and catch a killer, and today he found himself dressed as cupid and singing freaking love songs to love-struck strangers for Valentine's Day. He never thought he'd see the day. He glanced at Shannon as she kept pace at his side as they walked down the long narrow corridor toward her apartment door. Her small warm fingers wove perfectly with his.

He'd do it all over again if need be, dress as Santa and listen to a thousand whiny kids as they rattled of their Christmas lists. Dress as cupid and sing to love-struck starry-eyed people all day long. For crissake he'd dress as a freaking leprechaun and search the world high and low for a pot of gold at the end of a rainbow if she wanted him to. He was a hopeless case. He'd never be able to walk away from her on his own.

Fear shot though his veins. What would he do if she walked away from him? How would he ever get her to forgive him for the mess he'd caused today?

Shannon fumbled through her purse and surfaced with her apartment door key a moment later. Her hands shook as she tried to enter it into the key slot. Evidently the day had taken its toll on her. Though she was no longer engaged to Meyers, she once was close to him, and though she'd only dated the others for short periods of time, she had to be devastated by the mere thought that a crazy woman's jealousy of her had caused their deaths. Spinelli'd give his right arm if he could go back in time and change the events of the day. Shannon turned the key, but before she could open the door, the apartment door behind them opened. Mrs. Finch stuck her head out. "Is that you dear?" she asked as her thin-lipped smile stretched from ear to ear. "No doubt it is. I can tell from that glorious smell you have your handsome friend with you tonight as well," she added with a wink.

He liked Mrs. Finch. She was a sweet little old lady who was always happy and bubbly, just like Mrs. Knight, her sister, who lived with her. Though Mrs. Finch was nearly blind, it didn't seem slow her down any.

The shuffle of feet sounded behind Mrs. Finch. Mrs. Knight surfaced in the doorway as well. Not only were they identical twins, they still, after decades, dressed the same and wore their hair the same as well. The ladies stood before them wearing their plush looking pink bathrobes belted at their tiny waists. Their petite feet were covered in matching pink slippers. Curlers held their steel gray hair in place, their smiles resembled one another, and the sparkle in their eyes was identical.

Shannon smiled softly at her neighbors. "You ladies are up kind of late tonight."

The two women shared a giggle, and even that sounded the same. "We got caught up in the Johnny Carson marathon on TV. He's so funny. I just love when he plays that 'Carnac the Magnificent' character," Mrs. Finch beamed. She was the talker of the two.

A look of realization crossed Shannon's face. "Oh my gosh. I almost forgot. Happy Birthday. Hold on a second, I'll be right back," Shannon said as she disappeared into her apartment and returned a moment later with a bottle of Peppermint Schnapps in one hand and a bag of specialty Irish Cream coffee in the other. She handed the bottle to Mrs. Finch and the bag to Mrs. Knight. Though the women looked and dressed the same, the choice of Shannon's gifts to them made complete sense to Spinelli.

Spinelli stepped toward Mrs. Knight, leaned over, and gave her a little peck on the cheek, "Happy Birthday." He stepped toward Mrs. Finch and did the same. "So how old are you lovely ladies now, fifty?"

Mrs. Finch reached up and placed her cold, frail, bony hand on his cheek and gave it a little pat. "Always a charmer." She shifted her glance in Shannon's direction. "A real keeper this one." She turned her attention back to him. "And that would be ninety. A young ninety."

He was shocked. He knew they were old, but he hadn't realized exactly how old. "Ninety," he repeated. "What's your secret?"

She patted him on the cheek again. "Good clean living and a shot of Peppermint Schnapps over ice every night right before you go to bed." She winked. "It keeps the pipes fresh."

He couldn't help but chuckle. Perhaps he should give it a try.

Mrs. Knight reached into her pocket, pulled out a piece of paper, and handed it to Shannon. "Can you pick these up for us tomorrow?"

Spinelli caught a glimpse of the note. It was their grocery list. Shannon acted as their caretaker. The poor old ladies had no one else, but Shannon didn't seem to mind. Her sweet, caring nature was just one of the many things he loved about her, proving once again she was just too good for him.

Shannon glanced at the list. "Absolutely. Not a problem."

"Great," Mrs. Knight replied before she reached over and tugged on her sister's arm. "Come on Sister, it's late. Time to let these kids get on with their Valentine's evening."

Spinelli wished the ladies goodnight before they headed back into their apartment. Then he turned toward Shannon. "This has been quite the day. You must be exhausted."

She simply nodded. Her big green eyes grabbed hold of him. He couldn't seem to move. He knew he needed to leave right this second. If he didn't, he wouldn't be able to, and he'd just prolong the inevitable— the fact that he couldn't burden her with himself. The thought made him sick, but he needed to be strong and do it for her. It was for the best.

His feet made a slight shift forward, almost as if they had a mind of their own. He willed them to stop. If he stepped any closer to her, he'd kiss her on her warm soft inviting lips. He loved her full lips, and her sweet tasting mouth, which over the past couple of months had become solely his for the taking, or so he'd thought.

He squeezed his eyes shut. He couldn't think. He was a selfish man. He wanted her so bad. He took a step back and realigned his thoughts. He needed to go—now. He expelled a breath. "Get some rest. I'll see you later."

He turned quickly and took a step while he still had the strength. It worked until he heard his name roll of her sweet tongue. His feet froze in place. Her hand came to rest lightly on his shoulder. An electrical current whipped through his veins, nearly knocking him over. It was the same sensation he'd experienced the first time she'd ever touched him. He remembered it vividly.

Don't turn around, Spinelli. Don't do it. Stay strong for her. You've caused her too much grief. She's too good for you. Be the bigger person here. Let her go.

He heard her sigh. "Nick, don't do this. I know what you're thinking, and it isn't true. You're not responsible for any of this. This was not your fault. Bethany did it. Not you."

He didn't budge. He tried, but his feet wouldn't move. And he felt relieved that she didn't know what he fully thought.

She squeezed his shoulder. "You're a good person, Nick. No matter what you think, I want you to know right here and now that you are the finest person I know."

Tears stung the back of his eyes. She had no idea what those words meant to him just now. Never in his life had anyone ever said anything like that to him. Having grown up on the wrong side of the tracks, nobody ever felt such things or stated them with such conviction.

He spun to face her. The sea of green staring back at him swallowed him whole. His heart fluttered. He was done. He reached toward her and pulled her to him. He pressed his lips to her soft moist mouth. Her arms wrapped around his neck. Her fingers wove through his hair. The soft touch of her fingertips sent his every nerve ending screaming for more attention. She parted her lips, inviting him in to her gorgeous, full mouth. He slowly caressed her tongue, savoring her sweet taste and every moment as if it were his last.

He reached out and pushed her apartment door open and eased her inside without breaking contact. He was sure he wouldn't be able to separate his lips from hers even if he'd tried. He kicked the door shut behind him and eased her backwards through the living room, down the hall and into her bedroom. His hungry mouth never leaving hers. His tongue exploring every inch of her mouth seeking out every last bit of her tantalizing flavor.

Finally, the magnetism of their lips lightened, and he pulled his lips from hers. She stood before him wearing nothing but red silk panties, a matching pushup bra, and her tall red boots. His heart skipped a beat. He loved her undergarments. They were nothing like the conservative clothing she wore on the outside; always so prim and proper at work.

He eyed her. She had the most beautiful body. Her pale skin contrasted to what little red clothing remained on her. His thoughts shifted to the purchase he'd made earlier in the day at Madam Layla's Lingerie Shop. The package containing the hot pink fur-lined garment, wrist cuffs, and rose tipped whip lay on the seat of his truck. His examined her again. He didn't need the package. All he needed was her.

He reached toward her and in one quick flick of his finger and thumb the soft silky garment holding her breasts in place flung open, releasing her pale-skinned, perky breasts. They bounced slightly. The small raspberry tips were already taut, waiting for his touch. His lips begged him to wrap them around the budded tips. His mouth watered copiously.

Almost as if she'd read his mind, she shrugged her shoulders free from the straps of her bra, and it floated to the floor then she reached up and pulled his head to her breast. He easily let her. His willing lips wrapped around her breast. His teeth tugged lightly at her nipple. He pushed his tongue against its stiff point. The rich fragrance coming off her skin intoxicated him. He needed more of her. His mouth drifted to her other breast and performed the same, slow, gratifying maneuver. A soft groan escaped her lips. His own pleasure grew from hers. His lips burned with delight.

He slowly worked his mouth upward until it reached the hollow of her throat. He ran his tongue over it. Her pulse fluttered against his tongue. He hadn't thought it possible to become more turned on or to fall deeper in love with this green-eyed angel, but the incalculable depth of intensity that rushed through his veins as her pulse thudded against his tongue proved him wrong.

He skimmed his lips upward, over her jaw, not stopping until he found her luscious mouth. He took possession of it, kissing her hard and deep. He swallowed her soft sigh. If he hadn't already been hard as a rock, the sound of her sigh stifled in his throat surly would have done the trick.

Shannon skimmed her small warm hands over his shoulders, down his back, and under the waistband of his boxers. The burning sensation that trailed her fingertips intensified with each passing moment. If she kept it up any longer, he'd probably burst into flames.

She pulled her lips from his, leaned over, and retrieved a condom from the drawer of her nightstand. He watched as her small fingers tore the package open. She'd better hurry.

Her tiny hands sheathed him. Oddly, her sheathing him was always the most erotic experience for him. His body begged for release, yet he knew he had work to do first. He willed himself to recapture his control.

He slid his hand under the slim waist band of her silky red panties and slowly dragged them down her legs. She stepped out of them. She still wore her tall, red, spike-heeled boots. She reached for the zipper of her boot. He grabbed her hand. "Leave them on," he whispered. He wanted to feel the leather wrapped around him.

She smiled and nodded, then lay down on the bed.

He climbed in beside her and watched her as she slowly ran her tongue over her ruby red lips. He leaned toward her and claimed her mouth with his. All control was lost. He cupped her breast. It fit perfectly in his hand. He messaged both breasts before running his hand over her smooth flat stomach. He slid his hand down further, finding her wet and ready for him. Her throaty moan rang in his ears. He couldn't wait any longer. He was greedy, so greedy. He positioned himself on top of her and slid himself inside her. Her warmth surrounded him both physically and emotionally. It was as if madness overcame him. He drove deeper into her.

She met his every thrust. She wrapped her legs around him and hooked her heels together. The leather from her boots squeaked. He drove harder and deeper until she pulsated with pleasure around him. His own heated pleasure swept through him with more intensity than a wildfire. His release didn't take long to follow. He collapsed, totally spent.

He rolled off her and attempted to catch his breath. She rolled with him curling into the curve of his arm. Her warm hand rested on his chest. He placed his hand over hers. His thudding heartbeat penetrated through her palm and into his. He wondered if she had a clue as to the intensity of his feelings for her. They'd yet to exchange the "L" word. In fact, he'd never used it before. For some reason, he fought the urge to say it now. Why was he fighting it? He truly felt it. Why not say it? Fear swept through him. What if she didn't say it back? He'd feel like such an idiot.

Her breaths grew slow and even. Exhaustion finally consumed her. She'd fallen asleep. He couldn't blame her. She'd had a pretty tough day. Her silky red hair spilled over his shoulder and chest. He inhaled, capturing her scent. Her hair always smelled like a fresh spring morning.

The "L" word still lingered in his mind. Perhaps he should practice saying it now while she slept. What harm could come of that? It escaped his lips before he could think twice about it this time.

She lifted her head and met his gaze. Her eyes sparkled. "I love you too, Nick."

She brushed her full sweet lips softly across his and laid her head back down on his chest.

Relief swept through him. *That wasn't so bad.* His eyes watered. He'd never heard anything so beautiful and satisfying in his life. His blurry gaze shifted to his jeans on the floor in the bedroom doorway. He thought about the ring in his pocket. He glanced at the clock, two minutes to midnight, still Valentine's Day. He still had time to do what he'd set out to do on this particular day.

About the Author

Valerie Clarizio lives in beautiful Door County Wisconsin with her husband and extremely spoiled cat. She loves to read, write, and spend time at her cabin in the Upper Peninsula of Michigan. She's lived her life surrounded by men, three brothers, a husband, and a male Siamese cat who required his own instruction manual. Keeping up with all the men in her life has turned her into a successful hunter and fisherwoman. She holds a Master of Business Administration degree and works as a Finance Director. She is a member of Romance Writers of America and the Wisconsin Romance Writers of America.

Twitter:@VClarizio
http://www.facebook.com/val.clarizio
http://valclarizio.wordpress.com/

Other works by the author with Melange Books

Covert Exposure, A Nick Spinelli Mystery

www.ingramcontent.com/pod-product-compliance
Lightning Source LLC
Chambersburg PA
CBHW031842170626
46807CB00004B/1576